THE BOY
TRAPPER

HARRY CASTLEMON

1st WORLD
LIBRARY
Literary Society

The Boy Trapper

Harry Castlemon

© 1st World Library – Literary Society, 2006
PO Box 2211
Fairfield, IA 52556
www.1stworldlibrary.org
First Edition

LCCN: 2006905710

Softcover ISBN: 1-4218-2139-7
Hardcover ISBN: 1-4218-2039-0
eBook ISBN: 1-4218-2239-3

Purchase *"The Boy Trapper"*
as a traditional bound book at:
www.1stWorldLibrary.org/purchase.asp?ISBN=1-4218-2139-7

1st World Library Literary Society is a nonprofit
organization dedicated to promoting literacy by:

- Creating a free internet library accessible from any
  computer worldwide.
- Hosting writing competitions and offering book
  publishing scholarships.

The Boy Trapper
contributed by Tim, Ed & Rodney
in support of
1st World Library Literary Society

CONTENTS

CHAPTER I

A GLANCE AT THE PAST

"Don't worry about it, mother. It is nothing we can help."

"It seems to me that I might have helped it. If I had gone to General Gordon when your father first spoke about that barrel with the eighty thousand dollars in it, and told him the whole story, things might have turned out differently. But in spite of all he said, I did not suppose that he was in earnest."

"Neither did I. That any man in his sober senses should think of such a thing! Why, mother, if there had been so much money buried in that potato-patch, the General would have known it, and don't you suppose he would have found it if he'd had to plough the field up ten feet deep? Of course he would."

"But just think of the disgrace that has been brought upon us."

"Father is the only one who has done anything to be ashamed of, and he made matters worse by running away. If he would come home and attend to his business, no one would say a word to him. The General told me so this morning."

"I am afraid you couldn't make your father believe it."

"Perhaps not, but if I knew where to find him I should try."

It was David Evans who spoke last. He and his mother were talking over the strange incidents that had happened in the settlement during the last few days, and which we have attempted to describe in the preceding volume of this series. The events were brought about by a very foolish notion which Godfrey Evans, David's father, suddenly got into his head.

During our late war it was the custom of the people living in the South to conceal their valuables when they heard of the approach of the Union army. They were also careful to take the same precautions to save their property when it became known that the rebel guerillas were near at hand; for these worthies were oftentimes but little better than organized bands of robbers, and the people stood as much in fear of them as they did of the Federals. These valuables, consisting for the most part of money, jewelry and silverware, were sometimes hidden in cellars, in hollow logs in the woods and in barns; but more frequently they were buried in the ground. The work of hiding them was sometimes performed by the planters themselves, if they happened to be at home, but it was generally intrusted to old and faithful servants in whom their owners had every confidence. It not unfrequently happened that these old and faithful servants proved themselves utterly unworthy of the trust reposed in them. Sometimes they told the raiding soldiers where the property was concealed, and at others they ran away without telling even their masters where the valuables were hidden. General Gordon's old servant, Jordan, was one of this stamp. He went off with the Union forces, who raided that part of Mississippi, and before he went he told a rebel soldier, Godfrey Evans, who happened to be at home on a furlough, and who was skulking in the woods to avoid capture, that he had just buried a barrel containing eighty thousand dollars in gold and silver in his master's potato-patch, and that none of the family knew where it was.

This Godfrey Evans had been well off in the world at one time. He had property to the amount of fifteen thousand dollars; but, like many others, he lost it all during the war, and returned home after the surrender of General Lee to find himself a poor man. His comfortable house had been burned over the heads of his wife and children, who were now living in a rude hut which some kind-hearted neighbors had hastily erected; his negroes, who had made his money for him, were all gone; his cattle had been slaughtered by both rebel and Union troops, and his mules and horses carried off; his fine drove of hogs, which ran loose in the woods, and upon which he relied to furnish his year's supply of bacon, had wandered away and become wild; and Godfrey had nothing but his rifle and his two hands with which to begin the world anew. But it was hard to go back and begin again where he had begun forty years ago. The bare thought of it was enough to discourage Godfrey, who declared that he wouldn't do it, and made his words good by becoming a roving vagabond. He spent the most of his time at the landing, watching the steamers as they came in, and the rest in wandering listlessly about the woods, shooting just game enough to keep him in powder, lead and tobacco. His sole companion and friend was his son Daniel, who, being a chip of the old block, faithfully imitated his father's lazy, useless mode of life. Mrs. Evans and the younger son, David, were the only members of the family who worked. They never lost an opportunity to turn an honest penny, and there were times when Godfrey and Dan would have gone supperless to bed if it had not been for these two faithful toilers.

Godfrey disliked this aimless, joyless existence as much as he disliked work, and even Dan at times longed for something better. They both wanted to be rich. Godfrey wanted to see his fine plantation, which was now abandoned to briers and cane, cultivated as it used to be; while it was Dan's ambition to have two or three painted boats in the lake, to have a pointer following at his heels, and to do his shooting with a double-barrel gun that "broke in two in the middle." He wanted to take his morning's exercise on a spotted pony - a circus horse, he called it; and to wear a broadcloth suit, a Panama hat and patent leather boots, when he went to church on Sundays. Don and Bert Gordon had all these aids to happiness, and they were the jolliest fellows he had ever seen - always laughing, singing or whistling. Dan thought he would be happy too, if he could only have so many fine things to call his own, but he could see no way to get them, and that made him angry. He hated Don and Bert so heartily that he could never look at them without wishing that some evil might befall them. He threatened to steal their horses, shoot their dogs, sink their boats, and do a host of other desperate things, believing that in this way he could render the two happy brothers as miserable as he was himself.

Godfrey and Dan lived in a most unenviable frame of mind for a year or more, and then the former one day happened to think of the barrel which old Jordan had told him was hidden in the potato-patch. He spoke of it while the family were at dinner, and announced that he and Dan would begin the work of unearthing the BURIED TREASURE that very night. If they didn't find it the first time they tried, they would go the next night; and they would keep on digging until they obtained possession of it, if they had to dig up the whole state of Mississippi. Dan almost went wild over the news. He and his father spent a few minutes in building air-castles, and then Godfrey, who felt as rich as though he already had the money in his possession, hurried down to the landing, entered the store there and called for a plug of tobacco, which the merchant refused to give him until he showed that he had twenty-five cents to pay for it.

Although Dan and his father had great expectations, which they believed would very soon be realized, they did not neglect to pay attention to small matters, and to pick up any stray dollars that chanced to fall in their way. David was a famous dog-breaker, and Don Gordon had offered him ten dollars to train a pointer for him. The offer was made in the presence of Dan and his father, and the former at once laid his plans to obtain possession of a portion of the money. While the two were on their way to the landing, where a shooting-match was to be held that afternoon, Dan stopped at General Gordon's barn, and having borrowed a shovel, with which to dig up the buried treasure, he went to the house, where he found Bert reading a book. He told him that David had sent him there after five dollars, as he wished to buy a new dress for his mother, and Bert, although he was well aware that, according to the agreement his brother had made with David, the money was not to be paid until the pointer was thoroughly broken for the field, advanced him the amount he requested. Arriving at the landing, Dan got the bill changed for notes of smaller denomination, and, while he was picking up his money, was surprised by his father, who was greatly amazed to see his son with such a roll of greenbacks in his hand. Knowing that Dan was too lazy to work - too much of a gentleman was the way Godfrey expressed it - he could not imagine where the money came from, and Dan refused to enlighten him on this point, fearing that if he did his father would go straight to Don Gordon and ask for the rest of the ten dollars. Godfrey urged and commanded to no purpose, and was obliged to be satisfied with the loan of a dollar, which he promised to return with heavy interest as soon as the barrel was found. He paid seventy-five cents of it for the privilege of entering as one of the contestants in the shooting-match, and the rest he used in purchasing the plug of tobacco for which the grocer had refused to credit him. He won nothing during the match, while Dan, to his father's great disgust, came in for one of the first prizes - a fine quarter of beef.

When the shooting-match was over, the father and son returned to the little hovel they called home. Dan at once put the mule into the cart and started back to the landing to bring home his quarter of beef; while Godfrey, by pretending to fall asleep on the bench in front of the cabin, was able to carry out a little stratagem that suddenly suggested itself to him. He knew that Dan was a thrifty lad in spite of his laziness, and that he believed in laying by something for a rainy day. He was never out of ammunition for his rifle, but he always took care to keep his little stock hidden away, so that his father could not find it. By watching him on this particular day, Godfrey was lucky enough to find out where the boy's hiding-place was. He went to it as soon as Dan drove away in the cart, and found there a goodly supply of powder, lead and caps, and also three dollars and twenty-five cents in money; all of which he put into his pocket.

Dan came back from the landing in due time, and his father, who had been calculating on having a good supper that night, was astonished to find that the beef had been sold. He was enraged at first, but when he learned that Dan had received three dollars and a half for it, he was quieted at once, and a happy thought came into his mind. He sent Dan into the woods to shoot some squirrels for supper, and while the boy was gone he went to the hiding-place and put back the ammunition and money just as he found them, believing that when Dan returned he would put the three dollars and a half there too. Nor was he mistaken. The boy presently came back with squirrels enough for supper, and as soon as he thought he could do so without being seen by any one, he went to his storehouse, and having made sure that the property he had already hidden there was safe, he added to it the sum he had received for the quarter of beef, and went away happy. His father was happy too for he had seen the whole operation.

Godfrey was too tired to dig for the buried treasure that night, so Dan went to bed as soon as it was fairly dark. His father waited until he was soundly asleep, and then went to the storehouse and took out all it contained. Dan's rage when he discovered his loss the next morning was something to wonder at. He knew where his property was, and he demanded its immediate return, threatening in case of refusal, to tell General Gordon about the barrel in the potato-field. This frightened Godfrey, who gave up the contents of his pockets, but not until he had forced Dan to tell him where he obtained the money he had seen in his hands at the landing the day before. He was astonished when he learned that it came from Bert Gordon, and set his wits at work to conjure up some plan, by which he might obtain possession of the rest. He went over to the General's at once, and there learned that Don and Bert had gone down to the landing with their father, where they were awaiting the arrival of two cousins, whom they were expecting from the North. Godfrey followed them there with all haste, sought an interview with Don, and by telling him some plausible story, induced him to advance the other five dollars. Godfrey hoped in this way to get the start of Dan and enjoy his ill-gotten gains all by himself, but Dan was there and saw it all, and his father, alarmed by the look he saw on his face, divided the money with him. Of course David knew nothing of this. He was saving those ten dollars for his mother. He did not expect to spend a cent of it on himself; and how he first learned of his loss and what was done about it, perhaps we shall see as our story progresses.

The two young gentlemen, Clarence and Marshall Gordon, for whom Don and Bert were waiting, and who landed from the steamer, Emma Deane, that morning, had been sent away from the city by their father, in order that they might be out of the way of temptation; but, as it happened, one of them ran directly into it. Clarence, the older, was anything but a model boy. He was much addicted to ale and cigars, and thought of nothing in the world so much as money. He was a spendthrift, and, like Godfrey Evans, had a great desire to be rich, but he never thought of working and saving in order to gain the wished-for end. This good old-fashioned and safe way was too long and tedious for him, and he was constantly on the lookout for a short road to wealth and consequent happiness. Before he had been twenty-four hours under his uncle's roof, he thought he had discovered it, and this was the way it came about:

Clarence and his brother arrived at the General's house in the forenoon, and before night came, the former wished most heartily that he had stayed at home. He was lonely and utterly disgusted with the quiet of the country, and the old-fashioned, prosy way his two cousins had of enjoying themselves. Music, horseback-riding, hunting, fishing and visiting made up the round of their amusements, and Clarence could see no fun in such things. As soon as it grew dark he slipped out of the house, and leaning over a fence that ran between the barnyard and a potato-patch, lighted a cigar and settled into a comfortable position to enjoy it. He had not been there many minutes, before he was startled by the stealthy approach of two persons, a man and a boy, who stopped a short distance from him and began digging with a shovel. Clarence listened to the words which the man uttered for the encouragement of the boy, who was doing the work, and was amazed to learn that there was a fortune hidden in that field, and that these two had come there to dig it up. In his eagerness and excitement Clarence leaned half way over the fence, puffing vigorously at his cigar all the while. The little round ball of fire glowing through the darkness caught the eye of the boy, who showed it to his companion, and the two, frightened almost out of their senses, took to their heels, leaving the eavesdropper lost in wonder.

Clarence was almost overwhelmed by the discovery he had just made. It was an opportunity too good to be lost, and he at once resolved that if there were eighty thousand dollars buried in that field, he must have a share of the money when it was brought to light. In order to bring this about, he must find out who this man and boy were. He had a very slight cue to guide him, but he followed it up so skillfully that by noon of the next day he knew as much about the eighty thousand dollars as Godfrey did, and had formed a partnership with that worthy, Dan being dropped as a useless encumbrance. They met, according to agreement, as soon as it grew dark. It happened that there was one who witnessed their interview, and heard all that passed between them, and that was Don Gordon, who had just returned from the landing, whither he had been to mail a letter to his cousin. Not finding the hostler about when he came back, Don attended to his pony himself, and was about to shut up the barn for the night, when he discovered what he supposed to be a thief prowling about. The lighted end of a cigar glowed through the darkness a moment later, and then Don saw that the prowler was his cousin Clarence. Greatly amused at his mistake, he was about to make his presence known, when it occurred to him that since Clarence had taken so much pains to get out of sight of the family, in order that he might enjoy his cigar, perhaps he would not like it if Don caught him in the act; so Don remained in his place

Harry Castlemon

of concealment, heard every word that was said when Godfrey came up, saw both of them get over the fence in the potato-patch, and followed and watched them while they were digging for the barrel.

Now, Don was one of the most inveterate practical jokers in the world, and the most accomplished one we ever saw. Godfrey had received more than one proof of his skill. He had been tripped up when there was no one near him; his hat had been knocked off his head by invisible hands, and he had seen horrid great things with eyes of fire staring at him from fence-corners, until he had become fully satisfied that the General's lane was haunted, and he would go a mile around through the fields before he would pass through it after nightfall. Here was another opportunity to frighten him, and Don knew just how to do it. Before he went to sleep that night, he had thought of something that beat all the other tricks he had heard of far out of sight.

CHAPTER II

DAVID'S VISITORS

The trouble began the very next morning. While Godfrey was sitting on the bench in front of his cabin, deeply engrossed with his own thoughts, Dan came rushing up with a face full of terror, and conveyed to him the startling intelligence that a "haunt" - a Northern boy would have called it a ghost - had been seen at General Gordon's barn. It looked exactly like old Jordan, the negro, who had buried the treasure in the potato-patch; but of course it couldn't be old Jordan, for he had never been heard of since he ran away with the Yankees, and everybody believed him to be dead. Godfrey listened in great amazement to his son's story, and, to satisfy himself of the truth of it, went up to the barn, with his rifle for company. He had not been there many minutes before he received convincing proof that Dan had told the truth, for he saw the object with his own eyes - a feeble old negro, dressed in a white plantation suit, and wearing a battered plug hat, who limped along in plain view of him, and finally disappeared, no one could tell how or when. That was enough for Godfrey. He started for home at the top of his speed, and scarcely dared to venture out of doors that night. He had an appointment with Clarence Gordon at dark, but he would not have passed that barn in his present state of mind, if he had known that he could make twice eighty thousand dollars by it.

Bright and early the next morning, Clarence came down to see why he had not kept his promise, and talked to him in such a way that Godfrey finally agreed to meet him that night, the boy promising to protect him from anything in the shape of a ghost that might cross their path. He kept his appointment this time, but he was sorry enough for it afterward, for the first object on which his eyes rested, when he and his companion reached the potato-field, was old Jordan, digging away as if he too were in search of the buried treasure. Godfrey would have taken to his heels at once, but Clarence, who did not believe in "haunts," walked up and seized the negro by the arm. After much argument, Godfrey was induced to do the same, and then his fears all vanished, for it was a veritable human being that he took hold of and not a spirit, as he feared it was. He declared, too, that the interloper was the missing Jordan, beyond a doubt, and that he had come there to steal the money he had buried in that same field years before. The negro was commanded to point out the spot where the treasure was hidden, but nothing could be learned from the old fellow. He would not speak at all, until Godfrey threatened to punch him in the ribs with his shovel, and then he denied all knowledge of the barrel. Upon hearing this, Clarence and his companion seized him by the arms, dragged him across the field, over the fence and down the road to Godfrey's potato-cellar, where he was tied to a stanchion with a plough-line and left with the assurance that he should never see daylight again until he told where the fortune was to be found.

Godfrey was stirring the next morning before it was fairly light, and the first sound that fell on his ears caused him to start and tremble with terror. He listened until it was repeated, and then started post haste for General Gordon's house. When he reached it, he found the whole plantation in an uproar. Don was missing and a search was being instituted. Clarence came out about this time, and Godfrey told him a most astounding piece of news. It wasn't old Jordan at all whom they had captured the night before, it was Don Gordon. Godfrey was sure of it, for he had heard him whistle as nobody in the world except Don Gordon could whistle. As soon as Clarence recovered from his amazement and terror, he mounted Don's pony and set out for the potato-cellar to see for himself. When he reached it, he found that the prisoner had already been liberated by somebody (it was Bert, who was guided to his place of confinement by Don's loud and continued whistling) and was no doubt on the way home by that time. What was Clarence to do? Of course he could not go back to the plantation and face his relatives after what he had done, and there was no other house in the settlement open to him. Just then he heard the whistle of a steamer coming up the river, and that settled the matter for him. He would go home. He jumped on the pony and was riding post haste toward the landing when he was waylaid by Godfrey Evans, who robbed him of twenty dollars, all the money he had in the world. As soon as he was released, Clarence made his way to the landing on foot, reaching it just in time to secure passage on the Emma Deane, pawned his watch for money enough to pay his way home, and finally reached his father's house in safety, only to be packed off to sea on the school-ship, where he remains to this day.

Don Gordon reached home with his brother's assistance, and has been a close prisoner there ever since, not yet having recovered from the effects of his night in the potato-cellar. Godfrey Evans is hiding in the swamp somewhere, fearing that if he comes home he will be arrested for three offences - robbing Clarence, assaulting Don, and trying to steal the eighty thousand dollars, which he still firmly believes to be hidden in the potato-patch. A week has passed since the occurrence of the events which we have so rapidly reviewed, and now that you are acquainted with them, we are prepared to resume our story.

"And if your father doesn't come back, how are we to live this winter?" asked Mrs. Evans, continuing the conversation which we have so long interrupted. "How is *he* to live?"

"His living will trouble him more than ours will trouble us," replied David, who, knowing that he was his mother's main dependence now, tried hard to keep up a brave heart. "It will be cold out there in the swamp pretty soon. I saw a flock of wild geese in the lake this morning, and that is a sure sign that winter is close at hand. Father had no coat on when he went away, and he was barefooted, too. And as for *our* living, mother, who's kept you in clothes and coffee, sugar and tea, for the last year?"

"You have, David. I don't know what I should do without you. You are a great comfort to me."

"And I'm never going to be anything else, mother. I never made you cry, did I? I ain't going to, either. I can take care of you, and I will, too. If I can't get work to do, I can hunt and trap small game, you know; and if I only had a rifle, I am sure I could kill at least one deer every week. That, reckoning venison worth six cents a pound, would bring us in about thirty dollars a month. Who says we couldn't live and save money on that?"

"But you don't own a rifle," said his mother, smiling at the boy's enthusiasm.

"Well, that's so," said David, sadly. "But," he added, his face brightening, "I shall have ten dollars coming to me as soon as Don Gordon's pointer is field-broken, and you shall have every cent of it. Besides, you haven't forgotten that I'm going to get a hundred and fifty dollars for trapping quail for that man up North, have you?"

"Have you heard from him yet?"

David was obliged to confess that he had not.

"He may have made a bargain with some one else before Don's letter reached him," continued Mrs. Evans. "You know this is not the only country in which quails are to be found, and neither are you the only one who would be glad to make a hundred and fifty dollars by trapping them."

"I know it, mother; but even if I can't get that job, I can get some other that will bring us in money," said David, who was determined to look on the bright side of things. "I'll earn another ten-dollar bill before the one I get from Don Gordon is gone, you may depend upon it."

With this assurance the boy kissed his mother and hurried out of the door, and Mrs. Evans, after clearing away the remnants of their frugal breakfast, also went out to begin her daily toil at the house of a neighbor. David made his way around the cabin, and was met by Don's pointer, which, coming as close to him as the length of his chain would permit, waited for the friendly word and caress that the boy never failed to bestow when he passed the kennel in which the animal was confined. The greeting he extended to his four-footed friend was a short one this morning, for David had other matters on his mind. He confidently expected that a few days more would bring him the wished-for order from the man who had advertised for the quails, and when it came he wanted to be ready to go to work without the loss of an hour; so he was spending all his spare time in building traps. He had four completed already, and just as he had got boards enough split out for the fifth, he heard the clatter of horses' hoofs on the road and looked up to see Bert Gordon and his brother ride up to the fence.

"Why, Don, I am glad to see you out again," exclaimed David, dropping his hammer and hurrying forward to greet his friend.

"Thank you," replied Don, accepting David's proffered hand. "I assure you I am glad to be out again, too. It's a fearful bore to be tied up in the house for a whole week, but I was bound to come down here this morning, if I had to come in the carriage, for I have news for you," added Don, putting his hand into the breast-pocket of his coat.

"Has it come?" asked David, in a voice that trembled with excitement.

"It certainly has. It was addressed to me, you know, and so Bert opened it. The man says, he wants fifty dozen live quails immediately, and - but there it is, read it for yourself."

Don produced the letter, and David took it with a very unsteady hand. A hundred and fifty dollars was a fortune in his eyes, a larger one too than he had hoped to earn for some years to come. He opened the letter and one glance at it showed him that the money was his, if he could only capture the required number of birds. They were to be trapped at once, the sooner the better, put into boxes, which were to be marked C. O. D. and forwarded, charges paid, to the address at the bottom of the letter.

"Cod," repeated David, whose opportunities for learning how business was transacted had been very limited, "does he mean codfish?" Don and Bert laughed heartily.

"No," said the former, as soon as he could speak. "C. O. D. means 'collect on delivery.'"

"O," said David, in a tone of voice which showed that he did not yet fully understand.

"It is nothing to be ashamed of," said Bert; "we didn't know what the letters meant until father told us."

"That's so," said Don; "how is a fellow to know a thing he has never had a chance to learn? Now when the birds are caught, you put so many of them in a box and on each box you mark the value of its contents. You send a notice of shipment to the man, and he will know when to look for the birds. When they arrive he pays the amount of your bill to the express agent, and the agent forwards it to you. You run no risk whatever, for the man can't get the quails until your bill is paid."

"Now I'll tell you what we'll do," said Bert, who saw by the expression on David's face that his brother had not made matters much clearer by his explanation, "you go to work and catch the quails, and when you have made up the required number, we'll help you ship them off."

"That's the idea," said Don. "We'll do anything we can for you."

"Thank you," answered David, who felt as if a tremendous responsibility had been removed from his shoulders.

"I'll write to the man to-day, informing him that you will go to work at once," added Don. "I don't suppose you could tell, even within a week or two, of the time it will take you to fill the order, could you?"

"I shouldn't like to make a guess," said David. "The birds rove around so that a fellow can't tell anything about them. They are plenty now, but next week there may not be half a dozen flocks to be found."

"Then I will write to him that the best you can say is, that you will lose no time. How does the pointer come on?"

"Finely," said David. "He works better than half the old dogs now. He's smart, I tell you."

"He takes after his owner, you see. I hope to get firmly on my feet next week, and if I do, I want to try him. Good-by."

"Now, there are two friends worth having," thought David, gazing almost lovingly after the brothers, as they rode away. "I don't wonder that everybody likes them. A hundred and fifty dollars! Whew! won't mother have some nice, warm clothes this winter, and won't she have everything else she wants, too?"

The boy did not see how he could possibly keep his good fortune to himself until his mother came home that night. His first impulse was to go over to the neighbor's house, and tell her all about it, but he was restrained by the thought that that would be a waste of time. He could make one trap in the hour and a half that it would take him to go and return, and the sooner his traps were all completed, the sooner he could get to work. His next thought was that he would let the traps rest for that day, go down to the landing, purchase some nice present for his mother and surprise her with it when she came home. Of course he had no money to pay for it, but what did that matter? Silas Jones was always willing to trust anybody whom he knew to be reliable, and when he learned that his customer would have a hundred and fifty dollars of his own in a few weeks, he would surely let him have a warm dress or a pair of shoes. When his money came he would get his mother something fine to wear to church; and, while he was about it, wouldn't it be a good plan for him to send to Memphis for a nice hunting outfit and a few dozen steel traps? Like his father, when he first thought of the barrel with the eighty thousand dollars in it, David looked upon himself as rich already; and if he had attempted to carry out all the grand ideas that were continually suggesting themselves to him, it was probable that his hundred and fifty dollars would be gone before he had earned them.

"Halloo, there!" shouted a voice.

David looked up and saw another horseman standing beside the fence - Silas Jones, who kept the store at the landing, and the very man of whom he had been thinking but a moment before.

"Come here, David," continued Silas. "I am out collecting bills, and I thought I would ride around and see if you have heard anything of that respected father of yours during the last few days."

"No, sir; we haven't," answered David, hanging his head.

"Well, I suppose you know that he owes me eight dollars, don't you?" said Silas.

"I knew he owed you something, but I didn't think it was as much as that," replied David, opening his eyes. In his estimation, eight dollars was a debt of some magnitude.

"That's the amount, as sure as you live, and if I had charged him as much as I charge others, it would have been more. I made a little reduction to him, because I knew that he didn't own more of this world's goods than the law allows. What is to be done about it? Am I to lose my money because he has run away?"

"O, no," said David, quickly. "I'll pay it, and be glad to do so. We may want groceries some time, you know, when we have no money to pay for them."

"That's the way to talk. Pay up promptly and your credit will always be good."

"All I ask of you," continued David, "is that you will wait about a month longer, until -"

"Can't do it; can't possibly do it," exclaimed Silas, shaking his head and waving his hands up and down in the air. "Must have money to-day. My creditors are pushing me, and I must push everybody whose name is on my books."

"But my name isn't on your books."

"Your father's is, and if you have any honor about you, you will see the debt paid."

"That's what I mean to do, but I can't pay it now."

"Can't wait a single day," said Silas. "If the money isn't forthcoming at once, you can't get a single thing at my store from this time forward, unless you have the cash to plank right down on the counter."

"I have always paid you for everything I have bought of you," said David, with some spirit.

"I know it; but your father hasn't, and if you want me to show you any favors, you will pay that debt to-day. You have always been called an honest boy, and if you want to keep that reputation, you had better be doing something."

So saying, Silas wheeled his horse and rode away, leaving David lost in wonder.

CHAPTER III

AN OFFER OF PARTNERSHIP

This was the first time David had ever heard that a son could be held responsible for debts contracted by his father. At first he did not believe it; but Silas seemed to think it could be done, and he was a business man and ought to know what he was talking about. The truth of the matter was, that Silas Jones was a hard one to deal with. He wanted every cent that was due him and more too, if he could get it. It made no difference how poor his customers were, he always found means to make them pay the bills they contracted at his store. The eight dollars that Godfrey owed him looked almost as large in his eyes as it did in David's. He could not bear to lose it, and he did not care what tricks he resorted to to get it. When he rode away he took all David's peace of mind with him, "Wasn't it lucky that I didn't go down to his store and ask him to trust me for a dress for mother?" thought the boy; as he picked up his hammer and resumed work upon his trap. "He would have refused me sure. Now there is only one way I can pay that debt, and that is to ask Don Gordon for the ten dollars he promised to give me for breaking his pointer. That's something I don't like, for the money isn't fairly earned yet, but I don't see what else I can do. Mother must have something to eat, and the only way I can get it is by making a friend of Silas by paying him this debt father owes him. I don't care for myself, and as for Dan - let him look out for number one. That's what he makes me do."

Harry Castlemon

While David was soliloquising in this way he heard a footstep near him, and looking up saw his brother Dan, whose appearance and actions surprised him not a little. His face wore a smile instead of the usual scowl, he had no coat on, his sleeves were rolled up, and he carried a frow in one hand (a frow is a sharp instrument used for splitting out shingles), and a heavy mallet in the other. He really looked as if he had made up his mind to go to work, and David could not imagine what had happened to put such an idea into his head. He stopped on the way to speak to the pointer and give him a friendly pat, and that was another thing that surprised his brother. Dan would have acted more like himself if he had given the animal a kick.

"He's up to something," thought David. "He wouldn't act that way if he wasn't. I shouldn't wonder if he wants part of that money I am going to get from Don Gordon, but he needn't waste his breath in asking for it. Every cent of it goes into mother's hands."

"Halloo, Davy!" said Dan, cheerfully. "I thought mebbe you wouldn't care if I should come out and lend you a hand. I hain't got nothing much to do this morning."

David made no reply. He was waiting to hear what object his brother had in view in offering his assistance, and he knew it would all be made plain to him in a few minutes.

"You got a heap of traps to build, hain't you?" continued Dan. "When be you goin' to set 'em?"

"I am going to set some of them to-night," was David's reply.

"Fifty dozen is a heap of birds, ain't it?" said Dan.

"How do you happen to know anything about it?" demanded David, who was greatly astonished.

"I heerd you an' Don talkin' about it."

"Where were you at the time?"

"O, I was around," answered Dan, who did not care to confess that he had intentionally played the part of eavesdropper.

David was silent, for he wanted to think about it. Here was another piece of ill luck. His experience had taught him that if he wished to make his enterprise successful, he must keep it from the knowledge of his father and Dan. If they found out that he expected to earn so much money, they would insist on a division of the spoils, and if their demand was not complied with, there would be trouble in the cabin. He had no fear of his father now, but here was Dan, who was an unpleasant fellow to have about when he was crossed, and he seemed to know all about it. There were troublous times ahead; David was sure of that.

"What does that feller up North want with so many quails, anyhow?" asked Dan, as he placed one of the oak blocks upon its end and began splitting off a shingle with the frow. "He can't eat 'em all by hisself."

"No, he wants to turn them loose and let them run," replied David, with as much good nature as he could assume. "You see they had an awful hard winter up there last year, and the quails were all killed off."

"Wall, what does the fule want to let 'em go fur, arter he's bought 'em?"

"Why, he wants to stock the country. He belongs to a Sportsman's Club up there. He and his friends will have a law passed keeping folks from shooting them for two or three years, and then there'll be just as many birds as there were before."

"Is that the way them rich fellers does?"

"That's what Don says."

"It's mighty nice to be rich, ain't it, Davy; to have all the money you want to spend, a nice hoss to ride, one of them guns what breaks in two in the middle to do your shootin' with, an' shiny boots an' a straw hat to wear to church! I wish me an' pap had found that thar bar'l with the eighty thousand dollars into it. I wouldn't be wearin' no sich clothes as these yere."

"That's all humbug," exclaimed David. "The silver things that old Jordan buried, the spoons, knives and dishes, were all dug up again and are in use now every day. General Gordon never had eighty thousand dollars in gold and silver."

"Don't you b'lieve no sich story as that ar," replied Dan, with a knowing shake of his head.

"That's what the Gordons say, anyhow."

"In course they do; an' they say it kase they don't want nobody diggin' arter that thar bar'l. They wants to find it theirselves. How much be you goin' to get fur these quail, Davy? As much as twenty-five dollars, mebbe thirty, won't you?"

This question showed that Dan didn't know all about the matter, and David took courage. "Yes, all of that," he replied.

"More, I reckon mebbe, won't ye?"

"I think so."

"You won't get fifty, will you?" said Dan, opening his eyes.

"I hope I shall."

"Whew!" whistled Dan. He threw down his frow and mallet and seated himself on the pile of shingles, with an air which said very plainly, that with such an amount of money in prospect there was no need that any more work should be done. "That's a fortin, Davy. It's an amazin' lot fur poor folks like us, an' I can't somehow git it through my head that we're goin' to git so much. But if we do get it, Davy, we'll have some high old times when it comes, me an' you."

"You and me!" exclaimed David.

"Sartin; I want some good clothes an' so do you. 'Twon't be enough to get us a hoss apiece. I *do* wish I had a circus hoss like Don Gordon's, but we kin get some better shootin' irons, me an' you kin, an' mebbe we can git a boat to hunt ducks in, an' some of them fish-poles what breaks all in pieces an' you carry 'em under your arm. An', Davy, mebbe we'll have a leetle left to get something fur the ole woman."

"For mother! I rather think she'll get something," said David, in a tone of voice that made his brother look up in surprise. "She'll get it all, every cent of it."

"Not by no means she won't," exclaimed Dan, striking his open palm with his clenched hand. "No, sir, not by a long shot. You kin give her your shar', if you're fule enough to do it, but mine I'll keep fur myself. I'll bet you on that."

"*Your* share?"

"In course."

"I didn't know that you had any share in this business."

"Whoop!" yelled Dan.

He dashed his hat upon the ground, jumped up and knocked his heels together, coming down with his feet spread out and his clenched hands hanging by his side, as if he were waiting for an attack from his brother.

"No, sir," said David, quietly but firmly, "this is my own business. If you want money, go to work and earn it for yourself. You've got six dollars and six bits hidden away somewhere that you never offered to share with me or mother either."

"I know it, kase it is my own. I worked hard fur it too."

"I don't know how, or when you got it," answered David, who little dreamed that his brother had more ready money than that, and that the most of it rightfully belonged to himself, "and I have never asked you for any of it. The money I shall receive for these quails will be mine, all mine."

Dan uttered another wild Indian yell and once more went through the process of preparing himself for a fight, leaping high into the air, knocking his heels together, coming down with his feet spread out and his hands clenched, and when he was fairly settled on the ground again, he exclaimed:

"Dave, does you want me to wallop you?"

"No, I don't," was the reply; "but if you do you won't keep me from doing what I please with my own money."

"But it won't be your own when you get it. I'm older nor you be, an' now that pap's away I'm the man of the house, I want you to know, an' it's the properest thing that I should have the handlin' of all the money that comes into the family. If you don't go 'have yourself it's likely you won't tech a cent of them fifty dollars when it comes. If you don't go to crossin' me, I'll give you your shar' an' I'll take mine; an' we'll get some nice things like Don and Bert Gordon has got."

"But how does it come that you will have any share in it? That's what I can't understand."

"Why, I kalkerlate to help you set the traps an' take out the quail when they're ketched, an' do a heap of sich hard work."

"I intend to do all that myself, and it isn't work either. It's nothing but fun."

"But I'll have a shar' in it anyhow," said Dan, with a grin, which showed that he felt sure of his position, "kase look at the boards I've split out fur you."

David laughed outright. "How many of them are there?" said he. "Five; and I could have split them out in less than half the time you took to do it, and made better boards besides. I can't use these at all."

"Dave," said Dan, solemnly, as he picked up the frow and mallet, "I see you're bound to go agin me."

"No, I am not, and I don't want you to go against me, either."

"Yes, you be. You're goin' to cheat me outen my shar' of them fifty dollars, ain't you now?"

"You will have no share in the money. It will all belong to me, and I shall give it to mother."

"Then, Dave, not a quail do you ketch in these yere fields so long as you hold to them idees. Don't you furget it, nuther."

"What do you mean?" asked David, in alarm. "What are you going to do?"

"I don't make no threatenings. I only say you can't ketch no birds so long as you go agin me, an' that's jest what I mean. If you come to me some day an' say, 'I wus wrong, Dannie, an' now I'm goin' to act decent, like a brother had oughter do,' I'll give you my hand an' do what I can to help you. You've got a big job afore you, an' you can't by no means do it alone. You'd oughter have somebody to help you, an' thar's a heap of hard work in me, the fust thing you know."

"That's so," thought David, running his eyes over his brother's stalwart figure; "but I guess it will stay there."

We can make them fifty dollars easy, if we pull together; but you can't make 'em by yourself, an' you shan't, nuther. You hear me?"

As Dan said this he disappeared around the corner of the cabin, leaving his brother standing silent and thoughtful. He came out again in a few minutes with his rifle on his shoulder, and without saying another word to David or even looking toward him, climbed over the fence and went into the woods. When he was out of sight, David sat down on one of his traps and went off into a brown study. He was in a bad scrape, that was plain; and the longer he thought about it, the darker the prospect seemed to grow. He had his choice between two courses of action: he must either take Dan into partnership, divide the money with him when it was earned, and permit himself to be browbeaten and driven about as if he were little better than a dog; or he must make an enemy of him by asserting his rights. Which of the two was the more disagreeable and likely to lead to the most unpleasant consequences, he could not determine. If Dan were accepted as a partner, he would insist on handling all the money, and in that case Mrs. Evans would probably see not a single cent of it; for Dan did not care who suffered so long as his own wishes were gratified. If he stuck to the resolution he had already formed, and went ahead on his own responsibility, Dan would smash his traps whenever he happened to find them (he was always roaming about in the woods, and there was hardly a square rod of ground in the neighborhood that he did not pass over in the course of a week), and liberate or wring the necks of the birds that might chance to be in them. He never could capture so many quails if Dan was resolved to work against him, and neither could he make his enterprise successful if he allowed him an interest in it. David did not know what to do.

"I might as well give it up," said he to himself, after a few minutes' reflection. "I'll go up and tell Don that I can't fill the order; and while I am about it, I might as well ask him for that money. Perhaps, if I pay father's debt, Silas Jones will give us what we need until I can find something to do."

With this thought in his mind, David arose and went into the cabin. He put on the tattered garment he called a coat, exchanged his dilapidated hat for another that had not seen quite so hard service, and bent his steps toward General Gordon's house. While he was hurrying along, thinking about his troubles and the coming interview with Don Gordon, and wondering how he could word his request so that his friend would not feel hard toward him for asking for his money before it had been earned, he was almost ridden down by a horseman, who came galloping furiously along the road, and who was close upon him before David knew there was any one near.

"Get out of the way, there!" shouted the rider. "Are you blind, that you run right under a fellow's horse that way?"

David sprang quickly to one side, and the horseman drew up his nag with a jerk and looked down at him. It was Lester Brigham, one of the neighborhood boys of whom we have never before had occasion to speak. He was comparatively a new resident in that country. He had been there only about a year, but during that time he had made himself heartily detested by almost all the boys about Rochdale. Of course he had his cronies - every fellow has; but all the best youngsters, like Don and Bert Gordon and Fred and Joe Packard, would have little to do with him. He had lived in the North until the close of the war, and then his father removed to Mississippi, purchased the plantation adjoining General Gordon's, and began the cultivation of cotton.

Mr. Brigham was said to be the richest man in that county, and Lester had more fine things than all the rest of the boys about there put together. He took particular pride in his splendid hunting and fishing outfit, and it was coveted by almost every boy who had seen it. He had four guns - all breech-loaders; a beautiful little fowling-piece for such small game as quails and snipes; a larger one for ducks and geese; a light squirrel rifle, something like the one Clarence Gordon owned; and a heavier weapon, which he called his deer gun, and which carried a ball as large as the end of one's thumb. He had two jointed fish-poles - one a light, split bamboo, such as is used in fly-fishing, and the other a stout lancewood, for such heavy fish as black bass and pike.

If there was any faith to be put in the stories he told, Lester was a hunter and fisherman who had few equals. Before he came to the South, it was his custom, he said, to spend a portion of every winter in the woods in the northern part of Michigan, and many a deer and bear had fallen to his rifle there. He could catch trout and black bass where other fellows would not think of looking for them, and as for quails, it was no trouble at all for him to make a double shot and bag both the birds every time. There were boys in the neighborhood who doubted this. Game of all kinds was abundant, and Lester was given every opportunity to exhibit the skill of which he boasted so loudly, but he was never in the humor to do it. He seldom went hunting, and when he did he always went alone, and no one ever knew how much game he brought home.

"Your name is Evans, isn't it?" demanded Lester.

David replied that it was.

"Are you the fellow who intends to trap fifty dozen quail in this county, and send them up North?"

"I am," answered David.

"Well, I just rode down here on purpose to tell you that such work as that will not be allowed."

"Who will not allow it?"

"I will not, for one, and my father for another."

"What have you to say about it?" asked David, who did not like the insolent tone assumed by the young horseman. "Do the birds belong to you?"

"They are as much mine as they are yours, and if you have a right to trap them and ship them off, I have a right to say that you shan't do it."

"Why not? What harm will it do?"

"It will do just this much harm: it will make the birds scarce about here, and there are no more than we want to shoot ourselves. O, you needn't laugh about it, I mean just what I say; and if you don't promise that you will let the quail alone, you will see trouble. I am going to get up a Sportsman's Club among the fellows, and then we'll keep such poachers and pot-hunters as you where you belong. No one objects to your shooting the birds over a dog - that's the way to shoot them; but you shan't trap them and send them out of the country. Will you promise that you will give up the idea?"

"No, I won't," answered David.

"Then you'll find yourself in the hands of the law, the first thing you know," exclaimed Lester, angrily. "We won't stand any such work. Don Gordon ought to be ashamed of himself for what he has done. He's the meanest -"

"Hold on, there!" interrupted David, with more spirit than he had yet exhibited. "You don't want to say anything hard about Don while I am around. He's a friend of mine, and I won't hear anybody abuse him. He's the best fellow in the settlement, and so is his brother; and any one who talks against him is just the opposite."

Lester seemed very much astonished at this bold language. He glared down at David for a moment and then slipping his right hand through the loop on the handle of his riding-whip, pulled his feet out of the stirrups and acted as if he were about to dismount. "Do you know who you are talking to?" said he.

"Yes, I do," replied David, "and that's just the kind of a fellow I am."

Lester looked sharply at the ragged youth before him and then put his feet back into the stirrups again and settled himself firmly in the saddle. He felt safer there. "I'll be even with you for that," said he. "You shan't catch any quail in these woods this winter. I'll break up every trap I find and I'll make the rest of the fellows do the same."

Lester gave emphasis to his words by shaking his riding-whip at David, and then wheeled his horse and rode away.

CHAPTER IV

MORE BAD NEWS

David's feelings, as he stood there in the road, gazing after the retreating horseman, were by no means of the most pleasant nature. He was naturally a cheerful, light-hearted boy, and he would not look on the dark side of things if he could help it. But he couldn't help it now. Here was more trouble. If he had been disposed to give up in despair when he found that his brother was working against him, he had more reason to be discouraged when he learned that a new enemy had suddenly appeared, and from a most unexpected quarter, too. That was the way he looked at the matter at first; but after a little reflection, he felt more like defying Dan and Lester both. What business had either of them to interfere with his arrangements, and say that he should not earn an honest dollar to give his mother, if he could? None whatever, and he would succeed in spite of them. He would get that grocery bill off his hands the first thing, and when he was square with the world, he would go to work in earnest and outwit all his foes, no matter how numerous or how smart they might be. He would tell Don all about it and be governed by his advice.

Having come to this determination, David once more, turned his face toward the General's house. A few minutes' rapid walking brought him to the barn and there he found the boy he wanted to see. The brothers had just returned from a short ride - Don was not yet strong enough to stand his usual amount of exercise - and having turned the ponies over to the hostler, were on the point of starting for the house, when David came in.

"Halloo, Dave!" exclaimed Don, who was always the first to greet him. "Traps all built?"

"Not yet," answered David, trying to look as cheerful as usual.

"You have plenty of nails and timber, I suppose. If not come straight to us. It will never do to let this thing fall through for want of a little capital to go on," said Don, who was as much interested in David's success as though he expected to share in the profits of the enterprise.

"I have everything I want in the way of nails and boards," replied David, "but I - you know - may I see you just a minute, Don?"

"Of course you may, or two or three minutes if you wish. Come on, Bert. I have no secrets from my brother, *now*," said Don with a laugh. "I kept one thing secret from him and got myself into trouble by it. If I had told him of it perhaps he would have made me behave myself. Now what is it?" he added, when the three had drawn up in one corner of the barn, out of earshot of the hostler.

David was silent. He had made up his mind just what he wanted to say to Don, but Lester Brigham's sudden appearance and the threats he had made had scattered all his ideas, and he could not utter a word.

"Speak up," said Bert encouragingly. "You need not hesitate to talk freely to us. But what's the matter with you? You look as though you were troubled about something."

"I am troubled about a good many things," said David, speaking now after a desperate effort. "In the first place, there are two fellows here who say I shan't trap any birds."

"Who are they?" demanded Don, surprised and indignant.

"My brother Dan is one of them."

"Whew!" whistled Don, opening his eyes and looking at Bert.

"I didn't want him to know anything about it," continued David, "for I was certain that he would make me trouble; but he found it out by listening while I was talking about it, and wanted to join in with me. I told him I didn't want him, and he said I shouldn't catch any birds."

"Did he say what he would do to prevent it?" asked Bert.

"O, it's easy enough to tell what he will do," exclaimed Don. "He'll steal or break the traps and kill the quails. There are plenty of ways in which he can trouble us, if he makes up his mind to it."

"Who is the other?" asked Bert.

"Lester Brigham."

Don whistled again, and then looked angry.

"When did you see him, and what did he have to say about it?" he asked. "Has he any reason to hold a grudge against you?"

"I didn't know that he had until I met him in the road this morning. He says he won't have me trapping quails and sending them off North, because it will make them scarce here. He says he is going to get up a Sportsman's Club among the fellows, and then he will keep pot-hunters like me where we belong."

"Oho!" exclaimed Bert. "It seems to me that he is taking a good deal upon himself."

"That is what he has done ever since he has been here, and

that's why there are so many boys in the settlement who don't like him," said Don. "But he mustn't meddle with this business. He can't come down here into a country that is almost a wilderness and manage matters as they do up North. Father told me the other day that in some states they have laws to protect game, and it is right that they should have, for there are so many hunters that if they were not restrained they would kill all the birds and animals in a single season. The most of the hunters live in the city, and when they get out with their guns they crack away at everything they see; and if they happen to kill a doe with a fawn at her side, or a quail with a brood of chicks, it makes no difference to them. Sportsman's Clubs are of some *use* there, but we have no need of them in this country."

"He wants the quails left here, so that he can shoot them over his dog," continued David.

"O, he does! When is he going to begin? He has been here more than a year, and nobody has ever heard of his killing a quail yet. He must keep his fingers out of this pie. We can't put up with any interference from him. Any more bad news?" added Don, seeing that David's face had not yet wholly cleared up.

"Yes, there is," replied the latter, speaking rapidly, for fear that his courage might desert him again. "Just after you left me this morning, Silas Jones rode up and dunned me for eight dollars that father owes him."

"Why, you have nothing to do with that," said Bert.

"Nothing whatever," chimed in Don. "You tell Mr. Jones that if he wants his money he had better hunt up your father and ask him for it. You don't owe him anything, do you?"

"No, but he says that if I don't settle that bill, he'll never let me have a thing at his store again unless I have the money in my hand to pay for it. I haven't a cent of my own, and I thought if you could let me have the ten dollars you promised me for breaking the pointer, I should be much obliged to you."

"If I would do what?" asked Don, in amazement.

"Why, David," said Bert, "the money was all paid to you in less than twenty-four hours after the dog was placed in your keeping."

"Paid to me?" gasped David.

"Well, no, not to you, but to your order."

"To my order!" repeated the boy, who began to think he was dreaming.

"Yes, to your order," said Don. "We left the pointer in your hands at noon, while you were at dinner. In less than an hour afterward, Dan came over and said that you wanted five dollars to buy a dress for your mother, and Bert gave him the money. The next forenoon your father met me at the landing and told me you wanted the other five to buy some medicine for your mother, who was ill with the ague, and I gave it to him, and I just know I made a mess of it," added Don, bringing his hands together with a loud slap.

It was plain from the looks of David's face that he had. The boy listened with eyes wide open, his under jaw dropping down and his face growing pale, as the duplicity of which his father and brother had been guilty was gradually made plain to him, and when at last his mind grasped the full import of Don's words, he covered his face with his hands and cried aloud. Don and Bert looked at him in surprise, and then turned and looked at each other. They who had never wanted for the necessities, and who had never but once, and that was during the war, lacked the luxuries of life, could not understand why his grief should be so overwhelming; but they could understand that they had been deceived, and even the gentle-spirited Bert was indignant over it. The impulsive Don could scarcely restrain himself. He walked angrily up and down the floor, thrashing his boots with his riding-whip and cracking it in the air so viciously that the ponies danced about in their stalls.

"Dave," said Bert, at length, "are we to understand that your father and brother came to us and got that money without any authority from you?"

"That's just what they did," sobbed David.

"And you never saw a cent of it?"

"Not one cent, or mother either."

"Well, what of it?" exclaimed Don. "Brace up and be a man, Dave. A ten-dollar bill is not an everlasting fortune."

"I know it isn't much to you, but it is a good deal to me. You don't know what the loss of it means. It means corn-bread and butter-milk for breakfast, dinner and supper."

"Well, what of that?" said Don, again. "I have eaten more than one dinner at the Gayoso House, in Memphis - and it is one of the best hotels in the country - when corn-bread and butter-milk were down in the bill of fare as part of the dessert."

"Well, if all the folks who stop at that hotel had to live on it, as we do, they would call for something else," replied David. "How am I to settle Silas Jones's bill, I'd like to know?"

"Never mind Silas Jones's bill. If he says anything more to you about it, tell him that you don't owe him a cent."

"And how am I to send my quails away? That man said the charges must be paid."

"Ah! that's a more serious matter," said Don, placing his hands on his hips, and looking down at the floor.

"It is all serious to me," said David, brushing the tears from his eyes, "but I'll work through somehow. I'll go home now and think about it, and if I don't earn that money in spite of all my bad luck, it will not be because I don't try."

"That's the way to talk," said Don, giving David an encouraging slap on the back. "That's the sort of spirit I like. Bert and I will see you again, perhaps this afternoon. In the meantime we'll talk the matter over, and if we three fellows are not smart enough to beat the two who are opposing us, we'll know the reason why."

David hurried out of the barn, in order to hide his tears, which every instant threatened to break forth afresh, and Don, turning to the hostler, ordered him to put the saddles on the ponies again. "Father is down in the field," said he, to his brother, "and it may be two or three hours before he will come to the house. I can't wait so long, so we'll ride down there and talk the matter over with him. He hasn't forgotten that he was a boy once himself, and he will tell us just what we ought to do."

The ponies were led out again in a few minutes, and Bert, having assisted his brother into the saddle, mounted his own nag, and the two rode down the lane toward the field. Of course they could talk about only one thing, and that was the ill-luck that seemed to meet their friend David at every turn. The longer Bert thought and talked of the trick that had been played upon himself and his brother, the more indignant he became; while Don, having had time to recover a little of his usual good nature, was more disposed to laugh over it. He declared that it was the sharpest piece of business he had ever heard of, and wondered greatly that Godfrey and Dan, whom he had always believed to be as stupid as so many blocks, should have suddenly exhibited so much shrewdness. Bert declared that it was a wicked swindle; and the earnestness with which he denounced the whole proceeding made Don laugh louder than ever. Of course the latter did not forget that the trick which so highly amused him, had been the means of placing David in a very unpleasant situation, but still he did not think much about that, for he believed that his father would be able to make some suggestions, which, if acted upon, would straighten things out in short order.

"Well, Don, how does it seem, to find yourself in the saddle again? You appear to enjoy the exercise, but Bert doesn't. He looks as though he had lost his last friend."

This was the way General Gordon greeted his boys, when they rode up beside the stump on which he was seated, superintending the negroes who were at work in the field. Bert brightened up at once, but replied that he thought he had good cause to look down-hearted, and with this introduction he went on and told David's story just as the latter had told it to him and his brother. The General listened good-naturedly, as he always did to anything his boys had to tell him, and when Bert ceased speaking, he pulled off a piece of the stump and began to whittle it with his knife. The boys waited for him to say something, but as he did not, Bert continued:

"We came down here to ask you what we ought to do about it, and we want particularly to know your opinion concerning the trick Dan and his father played on us."

"That is easily given," replied the General. "My opinion is that Master Don is just ten dollars out of pocket."

"You don't mean that I must pay it over again?" exclaimed Don.

"No, I don't mean that, because you haven't paid it at all."

"Why, father, I -"

"I understand. Dan made a demand upon Bert, and Bert borrowed five dollars of his mother and gave it to him.

Godfrey came to you for the other five, and you gave it to him. David has not yet been paid for breaking the pointer."

"No, sir; but we supposed that his father and brother had authority to ask us for the money."

"You had no right to suppose anything of the kind. You ought to have paid the money into David's own hands, or else satisfied yourselves that he wanted it paid to some one else. Among business men it is customary, in such cases, to send a written order. You must pay David, and this time be sure that he gets the money."

"Whew!" whistled Don, who was very much surprised by this decision. "That will make a big hole in the money I was saving for Christmas; but David needs it more than I do, and besides it belongs to him. What shall we do to Godfrey and Dan? They obtained those ten dollars under false pretences, did they not?"

"I don't know whether a lawyer could make a case out of that or not," said the General, with a laugh. "I am afraid he couldn't, so you will have to stand the loss. Perhaps you will learn something by it."

"I am quite sure that I have learned something already," replied Don. "But now about Dan and Lester. How are we going to keep them from interfering with David?"

"Why, it seems to me that I could hide my traps where they would never think of looking for them, and where I would be sure to catch quails, too. If I thought I couldn't, I would set them all on this plantation, and any one who troubled them would render himself liable for trespass."

"Aha!" exclaimed Don, who caught the idea at once.

"But, in order to throw Dan off the scent entirely, you might have David come up to our shop every day and build his traps there. He will find all the tools he wants, and those shingles we tore off that old corn-crib will answer his purpose better than new ones, because they are old and weather-beaten, and look just like the wood in the forest. When I was a boy, I never had any luck in catching birds in bright new traps. When the birds are caught, he can put them into one of those unoccupied negro cabins and lock them up until he is ready to send them off."

"That's the very idea!" cried Don, gleefully. "We knew that if there was any way out of the difficulty, you would be sure to see it."

The General bowed in acknowledgment of the compliment, and the brothers turned their horses about and rode away. When they reached the barn Don was willing to confess that he was very tired. Riding on horseback is hard work for one who is stiff in every joint and lame all over; but Don could not think of going into the house and taking a rest. He had been a close prisoner there for a whole week, and now that he had taken a breath of fresh air and stirred his sluggish blood with a little exhilarating exercise, he could not bear to go back to his sofa again. He proposed that they should leave their ponies at the barn and go up to David's in the canoe. They would take their guns with them, he said, and after they had paid David his money, they would row a short distance up the bayou, and perhaps they might be fortunate enough to knock over a duck or two for the next day's dinner.

Bert, of course, agreed to the proposition, and went into the shop after the oars belonging to the canoe, while Don went into the house again after the guns. When he came out again he had a breech-loader on each shoulder and David's ten dollars in his pocket. Paying that bill twice did make a big hole in his Christmas money, for it took just half of it.

The brothers walked along the garden path that ran toward the lake, and when Don, who was leading the way, stepped upon the jetty he missed something at once. The canoe was gone.

They had not been near the jetty for a week, and the last time they were there the boat was all right. It could not have got away without help, for it was firmly tied to a ring in the jetty by the chain, which served as a painter, and even if that had become loosened the canoe would have remained near its moorings, for there was no current in the lake to carry it from the shore. Beyond a doubt, it had been stolen. Don would not have felt the loss more keenly if the thief had taken his fine sail-boat. The canoe was almost as old as he was, and in it he and Bert had taken their first ride on the lake and captured their first wounded duck.

"It's gone," said Don, after he and Bert had looked all around the lake as far as their eyes could reach, "and that's all there is of it. But we'll not give up our trip. We'll go in the sail-boat."

The sail-boat had been dismantled, and the masts, sails, rudder and everything else belonging to her had been stored in the shop under cover. While Bert was gone after the oars, Don drew the boat up to the jetty, and having stowed the guns away in the stow-sheets, he got in himself and took another survey of the lake to make sure that the canoe was nowhere in sight. It was hard to give it up as lost.

Bert came back in a few minutes, and having shipped the oars shoved off and pulled down the lake. A quarter of an hour afterward they landed on the beach in front of Godfrey's cabin. They found David wandering listlessly about in the back yard with his hands in his pockets; and when he came up to the fence in response to their call, they saw that he had been crying again.

"David," exclaimed Don, putting his hand into his pocket, "we've got news for you that will make you wear a different looking face when you hear it. After you went home, we rode down to see father, and he told us - Eh!" cried Don, turning quickly toward his brother, who just then gave his arm a sly pinch.

"Let me tell it," said Bert. "We'd like to see you at our house this evening about five o'clock; can you come?"

"I reckon I can," answered David. "Was that the good news you wanted to tell me?"

"No - I believe - yes, it was," said Don, who received another fearful pinch on the arm and saw his brother looking at him in a very significant way. "You come up, anyhow."

"We've got some work for you to do up there," said Bert. "It will not pay you much at first, but perhaps you can make something out of it by-and-by. It will keep you busy for two or three weeks, perhaps longer. Will you come?"

David replied that he would, and turned away with an expression of surprise and disappointment on his face. The eager, almost excited manner in which Don greeted him, led him to hope that he had something very pleasant and encouraging to tell, and somehow he couldn't help thinking that his visitors had not said just what they intended to say when they first came up to the fence.

"What in the name of sense and Tom Walker was the matter with you, Bert?" demanded Don, as soon as the two were out of David's hearing. "My arm is all black and blue, I know!"

"I didn't want you to say too much," was Bert's reply, "and I didn't know any other way to stop your talking. There was a listener close by."

"A listener! Who was it?"

"David's brother. Just as you began speaking I happened to look toward the cabin, and saw through the cracks between the logs that the window on the other side was open. Close to one of those cracks, and directly in line with the window, was a head. I knew it was Dan's head the moment I saw it."

"Aha!" exclaimed Don. "He had his trouble for his pains this time, hadn't he? Or, rather, he had the trouble and I had the pain," he added, rubbing his arm.

Bert laughed and said he thought that was about the way the matter stood.

CHAPTER V

DAN IS ASTONISHED

Many times during his life had David had good reason to be discouraged, but he had never been so strongly tempted to give up trying altogether and settle down into a professional vagabond, as he was when he left General Gordon's barn and turned his face toward home. He had relied upon Don to show him a way out of his trouble, but his friend had not helped him at all; he had only made matters worse by telling him more bad news. Nothing seemed to go right with him. There was Dan, who never did anything, and yet he was better off in the world and seemed to be just as happy as David, who was always striving to better his condition and continually on the lookout for a chance to earn a dollar or two. Why should he not stop work and let things take their own course, as his brother did? He reached home while he was revolving this question in his mind, and the first person he saw when he climbed the fence and walked toward the shingle-pile to resume work upon his traps, was his brother Dan.

"Whar you been an' what you been a doin' of?" demanded the latter, as if he had a right to know.

"I've been over to Don's house," answered David; "and while I was there I found out that you and father borrowed my ten dollars."

"'Tain't so nuther," cried Dan, trying to look surprised and indignant.

"I believe everything Don and Bert tell me. They have never lied to me and you have."

"Whoop!" yelled Dan, jumping up and knocking his heels together.

"I mean every word of it," said David, firmly. "You have got me into a tight scrape, but I'll work out of it somehow. And let me tell you one thing, Dan; you'll never have a chance to steal any more of my money."

"Then why don't you divide it like a feller had oughter do?" asked Dan, angrily.

"Why don't you divide with mother and me when you have some?"

"Kase I work hard for it an' it b'longs to me; that's why." And knowing by his past experience that he could not hold his own in an argument with his brother, Dan turned about and went into the house.

David worked faithfully at his traps, paying no further heed to his brother's movements. He tried to keep his mind on what he was doing, but now and then the recollection of the heavy loss he had sustained would come back to him with overwhelming force and the tears would start to his eyes in spite of all he could do to prevent it. Then he would throw down his hammer and wander about with his hands in his pockets, wondering what was the use of trying to do anything or be anybody while things were working so strongly against him.

It was during one of these idle periods that Don and Bert came up. David's hopes arose immediately when he caught sight of Don's smiling face, for he was sure that he was about to hear something encouraging. Indeed, Don's first words confirmed this impression; but it turned out that they had come there simply to offer him work that would keep him busy for two or three weeks. Of course David wanted work, but just then he wanted money more. He wanted to pay that grocery bill, so that he could look Silas Jones in the face the next time he met him.

When the brothers got into their boat and rowed away, David went back to his traps, while Dan, who had been disappointed in his hopes of hearing some private conversation between the visitors and his brother, shouldered his rifle and disappeared in the woods.

David worked away industriously until the sun told him that it was nearly four o'clock, and then he put on his coat and started off to keep his appointment with Don and Bert. He found them waiting for him at the General's barn, and he was not a little surprised when they seized him by the arms and pulled him into the carpenter-shop, the door of which they were careful to close and lock behind them.

"Now I know we can talk without danger of being overheard," exclaimed Don. "We've got lots to tell you; but in the first place," he added, opening his pocket-book, "there's your money."

The expression of joy and surprise that came upon David's face as he hesitatingly, almost reluctantly, took the crisp, new bill that was held toward him, amply repaid Don for the loss of the pleasure he had expected to derive in spending the money for Christmas presents.

"Why, I understood you to say that father and Dan had drawn this money," said he, as soon as he could speak.

"So they did, but my father says the loss is mine and not yours."

David drew a long breath. He understood the matter now. "It isn't fair that you should pay it twice," said he.

"I haven't paid it twice; that is, I haven't paid you at all. It's all right, David, you may depend upon it. They'll never fool us again. If I should ever have any more of your money, nobody could get it except yourself."

"Or mother," added David.

"O, of course. I wouldn't be afraid to trust her."

"I was in hopes that you would have a good deal of my money in your hands some day," continued David. "I was going to ask you to keep my hundred and fifty dollars for me; but I don't know now whether I shall ever get it or not."

"Of course you'll get it," exclaimed Bert. "You are not going to give up the idea of trapping the quails, are you?"

"No, but I don't know that I shall make anything at it, for Dan and Lester can break up my traps faster than I can make them."

"Well, they'll not break up a single one of your traps, because -"

Here Don began and hurriedly repeated the conversation which he and Bert had had with their father a few hours before. As David listened the look of trouble his face had worn all that day gradually faded away, and the old happy smile took its place. His confidence in his friends had not been misplaced; Dan and Lester Brigham were to be outwitted after all.

The traps and the "figure fours" with which they were to be set, could be built there in the shop, Don said. There were tools and a bench and everything else needful close at hand, so that the work could be done in half the time that David had expected to devote to it. As fast as the traps were completed they were to be set in General Gordon's fields. They would be safe there and Dan Evans or Lester Brigham or anybody else who came near them, would be likely to get himself into trouble. The negroes were always at work in the fields in the daytime, and if they were told to keep their eyes open and report any outsiders who might be seen prowling about the fences, they would be sure to do it. The best course David could pursue would be to say nothing more about trapping the quails. Let Dan believe that he had become discouraged and given up the enterprise. If he wanted to know what it was that took his brother over to General Gordon's house so regularly, David could tell him that he was doing some work there, which would be the truth; and besides it would be all Dan had any right to know.

As fast as the birds were caught, they could be locked up in one of the empty negro cabins; and any one who found out that they were there and tried to steal them, would run the risk of being caught by Don's hounds. It was a splendid plan, taken altogether, and David's eyes fairly glistened while it was unfolded to him. He thanked the brothers over and over again for their kindness and the interest they took in his success, and might have kept on thanking them if Don had not interrupted him with -

"O, that's all understood. Now, before you begin work on those traps we want you to help us one day. We've had a good deal of excitement and some good luck since we last saw you. We have recovered my canoe, which somebody stole from me, and we have found out that there is a bear living on Bruin's Island."

"He must be a monster, too, for such growls I never heard before," said Bert.

"Didn't you see him?" asked David.

"No. We landed to explore the island, and while we were going through the cane he growled at us, and we took the hint and left. We didn't have a single load of heavy shot with us. We're going up there to-morrow, and we want you to go with us. We'll go fixed for him, too. We'll have a couple of good dogs with us; I'll take my rifle; Bert will take father's heavy gun; and we'd like to have you take your single-barrel. If he gets a bullet and three loads of buckshot in his head, he'll not growl at us any more. If we don't get a chance to shoot him, we'll build a trap and catch him alive the next time he comes to the island. Will you go?"

Of course David would go. He would have gone anywhere that Don told him to go. He promised to be at the barn at an early hour the next morning, and then showed a desire to leave the shop; so Don unlocked the door, and David hurried out and turned his face toward the landing. He had money now, and that grocery bill should not trouble him any longer.

"If there ever was a lucky boy in the world I am the one," thought David, whose spirits were elevated in the same ratio in which they had before been depressed. "I'll earn my hundred and fifty dollars now, and mother shall have her nice things in spite of Dan and Lester. It isn't every fellow who has such friends as Don and Bert Gordon. But I shall have a hard time of it, anyhow. Dan will be so mad when he finds out that he can't ruin me, that he will do something desperate."

David, however, did not waste much time in thinking of the troubles that might come in the future. He preferred to think about pleasanter things. He was so wholly engrossed with his plans that it seemed to him that he was not more than five minutes in reaching the landing. There was no one in the street, and nothing there worth looking at, except General Gordon's white horse, which was hitched to a post in front of Silas Jones's store. As David approached, the General himself came out, accompanied by the grocer, who was as polite and attentive to his rich customers as he was indifferent to the poor ones.

"Ah, David!" exclaimed the General, extending his hand; "how are times now? Business looking up any?"

"Y-yes, sir," stammered the boy, who could scarcely speak at all. He was not abashed by the rich man's presence, for he had learned to expect a friendly nod or a cordial grasp of the hand every time he met him; but he was very much astonished by the greeting which Silas Jones extended to him. No sooner had the General released David's hand than it was seized by the grocer, who appeared to be as glad to see him as though he knew that the boy had come there to buy a bill of goods worth hundreds of dollars.

"It never does any good to give away to our gloomy feelings," said the General. "There are many times when things don't go just as we would like to have them, but the day always follows the night, and a little perseverance sometimes works wonders."

David understood what the General meant, but it was plain that the grocer did not, for he looked both bewildered and surprised. He bowed to his rich customer, as he rode off, and then, turning to David, conducted him into the store with a great deal of ceremony.

"Mr. Jones," said David, who began to think that the grocer must have taken leave of his senses, "I have come here to settle father's bill."

"O, that's all right," was the smiling reply. "It isn't fair that I should hold you responsible for that debt, and I have concluded that I will not do it. Your father will pay me some time, perhaps, and if he doesn't, I'll let it go. The loss of it won't break me. Can I do anything for you this evening?"

David was more astonished than ever. Was this the man who had spoken so harshly to him no longer ago than that very morning? What had happened to work so great a change in him? It was the General's visit that did it. When Don and Bert left their father, after holding that short consultation with him in the field, the latter took a few minutes to think the matter over, and when his hands had finished their work, he mounted his horse and rode down to the landing, to have a talk with Mr. Jones. What passed between them no one ever knew, but it was noticed that from that day forward, whenever David came into the store to trade, he was treated with as much respect as he would have been had he been known to have his pockets full of money.

"Want anything in my line this evening?" continued the grocer, rubbing his hands; "a hat or a pair of shoes and stockings for yourself, a nice warm dress for mother, or -"

"O, I want a good many things," replied David, "but I shall have only two dollars left after your bill is paid, and that must keep us in groceries for at least a month - perhaps longer."

To David's great amazement, the merchant replied: "Your credit is good for six months. As for your father's debt, I wouldn't let you pay it if you were made of money. Better take home some tea, coffee and sugar with you, hadn't you? It is always a good plan to replenish before you get entirely out, you know."

"O, we were out long ago," said David, who could not help smiling at the mistake Silas made in supposing that tea, coffee and sugar appeared on his mother's table every day. "We haven't had any in our house for almost a month."

"Is that so?" exclaimed the grocer, "Then I'll put up some for you, and lend you a basket to carry it home in."

David leaned upon the counter and began a little problem in mental arithmetic, with the view of ascertaining how much of his money it would take to keep his mother supplied with the luxuries the grocer had mentioned for one month, and how much he would have left to invest in clothing for her; but before the problem was solved the grocer had placed three neat packages, good-sized ones, too, on the counter, and was looking for a basket to put them in.

"Now, then," said he, briskly, "what next? A dress for mother or a pair of shoes for yourself? The mornings are getting to be pretty cold now, and you can't run around barefooted much longer. Ah, Dan! how do you do?"

David looked up and was surprised to see his brother standing by his side. He was surprised, too, to notice that the grocer greeted him almost as cordially as he had greeted himself but a few minutes before. David was not glad that he was there, for the expression on Dan's face told him that he had seen and heard more than he had any business to know. David made haste to finish his trading after that, and when he had purchased a dress and a pair of shoes for his mother, and a pair of shoes and stockings for himself, he handed out his ten-dollar bill in payment. Dan's eyes seemed ready to start from their sockets at the sight of it.

"Never mind that, now," said the grocer, pushing it back. "Perhaps you will need it some day and I can wait six months, if you are not ready to settle up before."

Dan's eyes opened still wider, and when his brother, after thanking the grocer for his kindness and confidence, gathered up his purchases and left the store, he followed slowly after him, so wholly lost in wonder that he never recollected that he had six dollars in his own pocket, and that he had come there to spend the best part of five of it. He walked along at a little distance behind his brother, looking thoughtfully at the ground all the while, as if he were revolving some perplexing question in his mind, and then quickened his pace to overtake him.

"Le' me carry some of them things," said he, as he came up with David.

"No, I thank you," replied the latter, who knew that Dan never would have offered to help him, if he had not hoped to gain something by it. "I can get along very well by myself. The load is not a heavy one."

"You're an amazin' lucky feller, Davy," continued Dan. "What you been a doin' to Silas, to make him speak so kind to us poor folks?"

"I haven't done anything to him. I don't know how to account for it, any more than you do."

"What's the matter, now? Forgot something?" asked Dan, as his brother suddenly stopped and looked toward the landing, as if he had half a mind to turn around and go back there.

Yes, David had forgotten something, and it was very important too, he thought. He knew that Dan was always on the lookout for a chance to make a penny without work, and David was afraid that he might be tempted to repeat the trick which he and his father had played upon Don and Bert with so much success.

It would be a very easy matter for Dan to make up some plausible story to tell the grocer, and perhaps on the strength of his brother's almost unlimited credit, he might be able to obtain a few little articles of which he stood in need. David had never thought to put Silas on his guard.

"I'll hold them things fur you, if you want to run back thar," said Dan, reaching out his hand for the basket.

"No, I'll let it go until the next time I come down," answered David. "A day or two will not make much difference."

"Whar did you get them ten dollars, any how?" asked Dan, as the two once more turned their faces homeward.

"That's the money you tried to cheat me out of," replied his brother. "Don says the loss was his and not mine."

"Did he give you ten dollars more?" exclaimed Dan.

"Not ten dollars more, for this is the first he has given me. You and father got what I ought to have had."

"An' you never spent none on it, did you? I seen Silas shove it back to you."

"Yes, I've got it safe in my pocket. I'm going to keep it, too."

"Wal, I'll bet a hoss you don't," was Dan's mental reflection. "I'd oughter have some on it, an' if you don't give it to me without my axin' you, I'll have it all. I'm the man of the house now, an' it's the properest thing that I should have the handlin' of all the money that comes in."

Of course Dan was much too smart to say this aloud. He knew that any threats from him would put his brother on his guard, and then he might whistle for the ten dollars. He said no more, and the two walked along in silence until they came to General Gordon's barn. Just as David was going into it, he met Lester Brigham riding out of it. Lester scowled down at him, but David did not scowl back. He was quite willing to forget that they had ever had any difficulty and to be friendly with Lester, if the latter wanted him to be. It is probable, however, that he would have had different feelings, if he had known what it was that brought Lester over to Don's house.

David, as we have said, turned into the barn, and Dan, who had more than his share of curiosity, would have given almost anything he possessed to know what business he had there; but he could not go in to see, for he dared not face Don and Bert after what he had done, so he kept on toward home.

David deposited his basket and bundles on the steps that led to the loft, and making his way around the north wing of the house, knocked at the door, which was presently opened by Bert. David asked if Don was in, and receiving an affirmative reply, was ushered into the library, where his friend, wearied with his day's exercise, was taking his ease on the sofa, which had been drawn up in front of a cheerful wood fire. David declined to accept the chair which Bert placed for him, and opened his business at once.

"Don," said he, "would you be willing to take that money you gave me and keep it until I call for it?"

"Of course I would," replied Don, readily. "You haven't paid that grocery bill, then? Well, I wouldn't either. You are not responsible for it."

"I offered to pay it, but Mr. Jones wouldn't take the money. He says my credit is good for six months."

"Why, what has come over him all of a sudden?" said Don, who did not know that his father had had an interview with Silas that very day.

"I wish I knew. There's the money, and you won't let anybody have it, except mother or me, will you?"

"You may be sure that I will take good care of it this time. Don't forget that bear hunt, tomorrow."

"No. I'll be on hand bright and early. Good-by."

David hurried out, and picking up the basket and bundles he had left in the barn, started for home. When he got there, he was surprised to see that Dan was at work. He had pulled off his coat, rolled up his sleeves and with a frow and mallet in his hands, was busy splitting out shingles. David said nothing to him, but went into the house to put away the tea, coffee and sugar and place the articles he had bought for his mother in a conspicuous position, so that she would be sure to see them, the moment she entered the door. While he was thus engaged, Dan came in smiling, and trying to look good-natured. David was on his guard at once.

"I'll tell you what I've made up my mind to do by you, Davy," said Dan, "an' when you hear what it is, if you don't say I'm the best brother you ever had, I want to know what's the reason why. I ain't goin' agin you like I told you I was."

"I am very glad to hear it," said David.

"No, I ain't. I'm goin' to be pardners with you, an' I'm goin' to give you half the money we make outen them quail. I'll give you half what I've got hid away, too."

"I have no claim upon that," replied David. "It belongs to Don Gordon, and if you are honest you'll give him every cent of it."

"I can't do it," said Dan. "Kase why, I give pap three an' a half of it, an' spent six bits myself."

"Then give him what you have, and tell him that you will hand him the rest as soon as you can earn it."

"Not by no means, I won't," said Dan, quickly. "Ten dollars ain't nothing to him."

"That makes no difference. It is his, and he ought to have it."

"Wal, I'll tell you what I'll do: I'll pay him outen them fifty dollars we're goin' to get fur them quail. An', Davy, if you'll give me the money you've got in your pocket, I'll hide it with mine whar nobody can't find it, and then it'll be safe."

"It is safe now."

"But if I go halves with you, you had oughter go halves with me. Let's go out to them traps agin, and we kin talk it over while we're workin'."

"I am not going to do anything more with those traps."

"You hain't give it up, have you? You ain't goin' to let them fifty dollars slip through your fingers, be you?"

"What encouragement have I to do anything after what you

said this morning? I have made other arrangements. I am going to work over at the General's."

David expected that his brother would be very angry when he heard this, but if he was, he did not show it. He looked steadily at David for a moment and then turned and walked around the corner of the cabin out of sight.

CHAPTER VI

BRUIN'S ISLAND

"That's a purty way he's got of doin' business, I do think. He's a trifle the meanest feller I ever seed, Dave is, an' if I don't pay him fur it afore he's a great many weeks older, I'll just play myself out a tryin'. If me an' him works together we kin get them fifty dollars as easy as fallin' off a log; but he can't arn 'em by hisself, an' he shan't, nuther."

This was the way Dan Evans talked to himself, as he trudged through the woods with his rifle on his shoulder, after his unsuccessful attempt to overhear what passed between his brother and Don and Bert Gordon; or, rather, after his failure to find out what it was that brought Don and Bert to the cabin. He *did* overhear what passed between them, but he did not learn anything by it. Of course that made him angry. A good many things had happened that day to make him angry, and he had gone off in the woods by himself to think and plan vengeance.

"Bein' the man of the house I've got more right to them fifty dollars nor Dave has," thought Dan, "an' if he don't give me half of 'em, he shan't see a cent of 'em hisself. Wouldn't I look nice loafin' around in these yere clothes while Dave was dressed up like a gentleman an' takin' his ease? I'll bust up them traps of his'n faster'n he kin make 'em. I'll show him that I'm the boss of this house now that pap's away, no matter if them Gordon fellers is a backin' on him up. I've larned a heap by listenin'. I heard Dave tell the ole woman that he's goin' to make three dollars a dozen outen them quail. I didn't larn nothing this arternoon, howsomever. Them fellers must a seed me lookin' through the cracks, kase they didn't tell him what they was agoin' to tell him when they fust come up to the fence."

Dan walked about for an hour or more, talking in this way to himself. The squirrels frisked and barked all around him, but he did not seem to hear them. He was so busy thinking over his troubles that he scarcely knew where he was going, until at last he found himself standing on the banks of a sluggish bayou that ran through the swamp. The stream was wide and deep, and near the middle of it and opposite the spot where Dan stood, was a little island thickly covered with briers and cane. It was known among the settlers as Bruin's Island. Dan knew the place well. Many a fine string of goggle-eyes had he caught at the foot of the huge sycamore which grew at the lower end of the island, and leaned over the water until its long branches almost touched the trees on the main shore, and it was here that he had trapped his first beaver. More than that, the island had been a place of refuge for his father during the war. He retreated to it on the night the levee was blown up by the Union soldiers, and spent the most of his time there until all danger of capture was past.

When Dan appeared upon the bank of the bayou a dark object, which was crouching at the water's edge near the foot of the sycamore, suddenly sprang up and glided into the bushes out of sight. Its movements were quick and noiseless, but still they did not escape the notice of Dan, who dropped on the instant and hid behind a fallen log that happened to be close at hand. He did not have time to take a good look at the object, but he saw enough of it to frighten him thoroughly. He thrust his cocked rifle cautiously over the log, directing the muzzle toward the sycamore, but his hand was unsteady and his face was as white as a sheet.

"Looked to me like a man," thought Dan, trembling in every

limb, "but in course it couldn't be; so it's one of them haunts what lives in the General's lane."

Dan kept his gaze directed across the bayou, and could scarcely restrain himself from jumping up and taking to his heels when he saw a head, covered with a torn and faded hat, raised slowly and cautiously above the leaning trunk of the sycamore. It remained motionless for a moment and Dan's eyes were sharp enough to see that there was a face below the hat - a tanned and weather-beaten face, the lower portion of which was concealed by thick, bushy whiskers. As Dan looked his eyes began to dilate, his mouth came open, and the butt of his rifle was gradually lowered until the muzzle pointed toward the clouds. He was sure he saw something familiar about the face, but the sight of it was most unexpected, and so was the sound of the voice which reached his ears a moment later.

"Dannie!" came the hail, in subdued tones, as if the speaker were afraid of being overheard by some one besides the boy whom he was addressing.

"Pap!" cried Dan.

As he spoke he arose from his concealment, and the man on the other side of the bayou - Dan was pretty certain now that it was a man - stepped out into view, disclosing the well-known form and features of Godfrey Evans. Dan could hardly believe his eyes, and even Godfrey seemed a little doubtful.

"Is that you, Dannie?" asked the latter.

"You're just a shoutin'," was the reply.

"Nobody ain't thar with you, I reckon," said Godfrey.

"No, I'm all by myself. But be you sartin that's you, pap?"

"In course I am, an' I've been a waitin' an' a watchin' fur yer. I'll bring you over. You're an ongrateful an' ondutiful boy to leave your poor ole pap, what's fit the Yankees an' worked so hard to bring you up like a gentleman's son had oughter be brung up, out here in the cane so long all by hisself."

"Why, pap, I didn't know you was here," said Dan.

Godfrey walked briskly along the shore until he reached a little thicket of bushes into which he plunged out of sight. He appeared again almost immediately, dragging behind him a small lead-colored canoe which Dan recognized the moment he saw it. It was Don Gordon's canoe, the one he used to pick up his dead and wounded ducks when he was shooting over his decoys. It was a beautiful little craft, and Dan had often wished that he could call it his own. It was one thing that made him hate Don and Bert so cordially, and he had often told himself that when he was ready to carry out the threats he had so often made, that canoe should be one of the first things to suffer. The brothers took altogether too much pleasure in it, and he wouldn't have them rowing about the lake enjoying themselves while he was obliged to stay ashore. The sight of it satisfied him that the man on the opposite bank was his father, and nobody else. If he had been a "haunt" he would not have needed a canoe to carry him across the bayou.

Having placed the canoe in the water Godfrey went back into the cane after the oars - the little craft was provided with rowlocks and propelled by oars instead of paddles - and in a few seconds more he was on Dan's side of the bayou. The moment the canoe touched the bank he sprang out, and if one might judge by the cordial manner in which father and son greeted each other, they were glad to meet again.

"I didn't never expect to feel your grip no more, pap," said Dan, who was the first to speak, "an' I'm ridikilis proud to see you with this yere dug-out. How came you by it, and whar did you git it?"

"I jest took it an' welcome," answered Godfrey. "I wasn't goin' to swim over to the island every time I wanted to go there, was I?"

"In course not. I'm scandalous glad you tuk it; an' now I'll have a ride in it, an' no thanks to Don Gordon nuther. Been a livin' here ever since you've been gone?" added Dan, as he stepped into the boat and picked up the oars.

"Yes, an' I've been a lookin' fur you every day. Seems to me you might a knowed where to find me, kase here's whar I hung out when the Yanks was in the country. Hear anything about me, in the settlement?"

"Yes, lots. Silas Jones has done been to Dave fur them eight dollars you owe him."

"Much good may they do him, when he gets 'em," said Godfrey, snapping his fingers in the air.

"Dave's goin' to pay the bill," added Dan. "I done heard him say so."

"The ongrateful an' ondutiful scamp!" exclaimed Godfrey. "If he's got that much money, why don't he give it to me, like he had oughter do? I need it more'n Silas does. Hear anything else, Dannie?"

"Yes; General Gordon says, why don't you come home an' go 'have yourself? Nobody wouldn't pester you."

"Does you see anything green in these yere eyes?" asked Godfrey, looking steadily at Dan. "That would do to tell some folks, but a man what's fit the Yanks ain't so easy fooled. I'm safe here, an' here I'll stay, till - Hear anything else, Dannie - anything 'bout them two city chaps, Clarence an' Marsh Gordon?"

"O, they've gone home long ago."

"You didn't hear nothing about them gettin' into a furse afore they went, did you?"

"Course I have. Everybody knows that you an' Clarence thought Don was ole Jordan an' shet him up in the tater-hole."

"An' sarved him right, too," exclaimed Godfrey. "I reckon he's well paid fur cheatin' me outen that chance of making eighty thousand dollars. I heard Clarence was robbed afore he went away," added Godfrey, at the same time turning away his head and looking at Dan out of the corner of his eyes.

"I didn't hear nothing about that," said Dan.

Godfrey drew a long breath of relief. Ever since he took up his abode on the island he had been torturing himself with the belief that the robbery of which he was guilty was the talk of the settlement, and that he would be arrested for at if he should ever show himself at the landing again. He breathed much easier to know that his fears on this score were groundless.

"Hear anything else, Dannie?" asked Godfrey, and his voice was so cheerful and animated that the boy looked at him in amazement. "What's Dave an' the ole woman doin'?"

"That thar Dave is goin' to git rich, dog-gone it," replied Dan, in great disgust. "He got a letter from some feller up North this mornin' tellin' him if he would trap fifty dozen live quail fur him, he'd pay him so't he could make three dollars a dozen on 'em. I seed Don give him the letter, an' I heard 'em a talkin' and a laughin' about it."

"That's what makes me 'spise them Gordons so," said Godfrey, slapping the side of the canoe with his open hand. "They're all the time a boostin' Dave, an' me and you could starve fur all they keer. Now jump out, an' we'll go up to my house an' talk about it. We'll leave the boat here, so't it will be handy when you want to go back."

As Godfrey spoke the bow of the canoe ran deep into the soft mud which formed the beach on that side of the island, and the father and son sprang out. Godfrey led the way along a narrow, winding path which ran through the cane, and after a few minutes walking ushered Dan into an open space in the centre of the island. Here stood the little bark lean-to that he called his house. The cane had been cleared away from a spot about fifteen feet square, and piled up around the outside, so that it looked like a little breastwork.

The lean-to was not a very imposing structure - Godfrey would much rather sit in the sun and smoke his pipe then expend any of his strength in providing for his comfort - but it was large enough to shelter one man, and with a few more pieces of bark on the roof and a roaring fire in front, it might have been made a very pleasant and inviting camp. Just now, however, it looked cheerless enough. There was a little armful of leaves under the roof of the lean-to and there was a block of wood beside the fire-place, the position of which was pointed out by a bed of ashes and cinders. The leaves served for a bed and the block of wood for a chair; and they were all the "furniture" that was to be seen about the camp. But Godfrey was very well satisfied with his surroundings and Dan was delighted with them. It must be splendid, he thought, to live there all by one's self with nothing to worry over and no work to do. It was not even necessary that Godfrey should chop wood for the fire, for the upper end of the island was covered with broken logs and branches, and five minutes' work every morning would suffice to provide him with all the fuel he would be likely to burn during the day.

"What a nice place you've got here, pap!" said Dan, when he had taken a hurried survey of the camp.

"I reckon it's about right," replied Godfrey. "I had this fur a hidin' place while the Yanks was a scoutin' about through the country, an' I come here now kase nobody won't think of lookin' fur me so nigh the settlement. An' they won't stumble onto me afore I know it, nuther. They can't git to me if they come afoot kase the bayou'll stop 'em; an' I never heard of nobody coming up here in a boat. Nothing bothers me 'ceptin' a bar. He comes over every night to feed on the beech-nuts an' acorns, an' some night he'll come fur the last time. I'll jest knock him over, and then I'll have meat enough to last me a month. I build my fire and do my cookin' at night, so't nobody can't see the smoke, an' that's what frightened the bar away afore I could shoot him."

"I've a notion to come here an' live with you, pap," said Dan.

"'Twon't be safe," replied his father, quickly. "If you're missin' from home folks might begin to hunt fur us, an' that's somethin' I don't want 'em to do. 'Sides you must stay in the settlement an' help me. I shall need things from the store now an' then, an' as I can't go and git 'em myself, you'll have to git 'em fur me. But what was you sayin' about Dave?" asked Godfrey, throwing himself down on one of the piles of cane and motioning to Dan to occupy the block of wood.

"I was a sayin' that he's a little the meanest feller I ever seed," replied Dan, "an' don't you say so too, pap? Kase why, he's goin' to git fifty dollars fur them quail, an' he's goin' to give the money all to the ole woman."

"An' leave me to freeze an' starve out here in the cane?" exclaimed Godfrey, with a great show of indignation. "Not by no means he won't. If he don't mind what he's about we'll take the hul on it, Dan, me an' you will."

"*He* won't get none on it, you kin bet high on that," said Dan. "I told him I was goin' agin him, an' so I am. I'll bust his traps as fast as I kin find 'em, an' I won't do nothin' but hunt fur 'em, day an' night."

"Now, haint you got no sense at all?" cried his father, so fiercely that Dan jumped up and turned his face toward the path, as if he were on the point of taking to his heels.

"Wal, I wanted to go pardners with him an' he wouldn't le' me," protested Dan.

"What's the odds? Set down thar an' listen while somebody what knows somethin' talks to you. What odds does it make to you if he won't go pardners with you?"

"Kase I want some of the money; that's the odds it makes to me."

"Wal, you kin have it, an' you needn't do no work, nuther. I'm Dave's pap an' your'n too, an' knows what's best fur all of us. You jest keep still an' let Dave go on an' ketch the birds; an' when he's ketched 'em an' got the money in his pocket, then I'll tell you what else to do. Le' me see: fifty dozen birds at three dollars a dozen! That's - that's jest -"

Godfrey straightened up, locked his fingers together, rested his elbows on his knees and looked down at the pile of ashes in the fire-place.

"It's a heap of money, the fust thing you know," said Dan. "It's fifty dollars. Dave told me so."

"Fifty gran'mothers!" exclaimed Godfrey. "Dave done said that jest to make a fule of you. It would be fifty dollars if he got only a dollar a dozen. If he got two it would be a hundred dollars, an' if he got three, it would be -"

Godfrey stopped, believing that he must have made a mistake somewhere, and stared at Dan as if he were utterly bewildered. Dan returned the stare with interest. "A hundred dollars!" he repeated, slowly. "That thar Dave of our'n goin' to make a hundred dollars all by hisself! Some on it's mine."

"It's more'n that, Dannie," said Godfrey, who, as soon as he could settle his mind to the task, went over his calculations again, adding the astounding statement -

"An' if he gets three dollars a dozen, he'll get a hundred an' fifty dollars for the lot."

Dan's astonishment was so great that for a few seconds he could not speak, and even his father looked puzzled and amazed. He was certain that he had made no mistake in his mental arithmetic this time, and the magnitude of David's prospective earnings fairly staggered him. It made him angry to think of it.

"The idee of that triflin' leetle Dave's makin' so much money," he exclaimed, in great disgust; "an' here's me, who has worked an' slaved fur a hul lifetime, an' I've got jest twenty dollars."

"Eh?" cried Dan.

Godfrey was frightened at what he had said, but he could not recall it without exciting Dan's suspicions; so he put on a bold face and continued: -

"Yes, I've got that much, an' I worked hard fur it, too. But a hundred an' fifty dollars! We must have that when it's 'arned, Dannie."

"The hul on it?"

"Every cent. I'm Dave's pap, an' the law gives me the right to his 'arnin's, an' yours, too, until you's both twenty-one years ole. Now, Dannie, I've done a power of hard thinkin' since I've been here on this island, an' I've got some idees in my head that will make you look wild when you hear 'em. I didn't know jest how to carry 'em out afore, but I do now. These yere hundred an' fifty dollars will keep us movin' till we kin find them eighty thousand."

"Be you goin' to look fur them agin, pap?"

"No, I hain't, but you be."

"Not much, I ain't," replied Dan, emphatically.

"Who's to do it, then?" demanded his father. "I can't, kase I'm afeared to go into the settlement even at night. You hain't goin' to give up the money, be you? Then what'll become of your circus-hoss, an' your painted boats, an' your fine guns what break in two in the middle?"

"I don't keer," answered Dan, doggedly. "I wouldn't go into that tater-patch alone, arter dark; if I knowed it was chuck full of yaller gold an' silver pieces."

The savage scowl that settled on Godfrey's face, as he listened to these words, brought Dan to his feet again in great haste. The man was fully as angry as he looked, and it is possible he might have said or done something not altogether to Dan's liking, had it not been for an unlooked-for interruption that occurred just then. Godfrey had raised his hand in the air to give emphasis to some remark he was about to make, when he was checked by a slight splashing in the water, accompanied by the measured clatter of oars, as they were moved back and forth in the row-locks. This was followed by a clear, ringing laugh, which Godfrey and his son could have recognized anywhere, and a cheery voice said: -

"I'm getting tired. It is time for me to stop and rest when I begin to catch crabs."

There was a boat in the bayou, and Don and Bert Gordon were in it. They were so close at hand, too, that flight was impossible.

"I don't think there's much difference between riding on horseback and rowing in a boat, as far as the work is concerned," said the same voice. "I've done about all I can do to-day. There don't seem to be any ducks in the bayou; so we'll stop here and take a breathing spell before we go back."

"Is thar any place in the wide world a feller could crawl into without bein' pestered by them two oneasy chaps?" whispered Dan, jumping up from his block of wood and looking all around, as if he were seeking a way of escape.

"Not a word out of you," replied Godfrey, shaking his fist at his son.

Following Godfrey's example, Dan threw himself behind one of the piles of cane, and the two held their breath and listened.

CHAPTER VII

WHAT HAPPENED THERE

"You're not going to get out, are you, Don?" asked Bert, and as he was not more than four or five rods away, every word he uttered was distinctly heard by the two listeners in the cane.

"I want to stretch my legs a little," was Don's reply. "Come on, and let's explore the island. You know it used to be a famous bear's den, don't you?"

"I should think I ought to know it, having heard father tell the story of the animal's capture a dozen times or more. He must have been a monster: he was so large and heavy that it was all a span of mules could do to drag him from the shore of the lake, where he was taken out of the boat, up to the house."

"And didn't he make things lively before he was killed, though?" said Don. "He destroyed nine dogs and wounded two men. I'd like to take part in a hunt like that."

"Well, I wouldn't. It looks gloomy in the cane, doesn't it? What would we do if we should find a bear in there?"

"I don't know," answered Don, with a laugh. "Our guns are loaded with small shot, and they would hardly penetrate a bear's thick skin. If he should come at us, I'd be a goner, sure, for I am so stiff I couldn't run to save my life. But I don't think we'll find - Halloo! Bert, just look here!"

A chorus of exclamations followed, and Godfrey and Dan looked at each other and scowled fiercely.

"That's my canoe," said Don, and they heard the oars rattle as he stepped into it.

"There's no doubt about that," said Bert, in surprised and delighted tones; "but how came it here?"

"That's the question. The fellow who stole it took it up the bayou and then turned it loose, having no further use for it, or else it got away from him and drifted down here."

"Who knows but the thief brought it here himself, and that he is on the island now, hidden in the cane?" said Bert, lowering his voice, but still speaking quite loud enough to make himself heard by Godfrey and Dan.

"I hardly think that can be possible," replied Don. "You see the bow of the canoe was caught on this root; and that makes me think it was brought down by the current and lodged here."

Godfrey and Dan looked at each other again. They had taken no pains to secure the boat when they left it, and the current had moved it from its place on the bank and was carrying it toward the lake, when it caught on the root where it was discovered by its lawful owner.

"I am glad to get it again," said Don, "for I don't know what we should have done without it. It is just the thing to chase crippled ducks with. If I could see the man who stole it, I'd give him a piece of my mind, I tell you."

After that there was a pause in the conversation and the rattling of a chain told Godfrey and Dan that the canoe was being fastened to the stern of the boat in which the brothers had come up the bayou. Then there was more conversation in a subdued tone of voice, and presently a commotion in the cane indicated that Don and Bert were working their way slowly toward the camp. Dan began to tremble and turn white, and his father looked as though he would have been glad to run if he had only known where to go.

"Halloo!" exclaimed Bert, suddenly, "here we are. Come this way, Don. I've found a path."

"A path!" repeated his brother. "What should make a path through this cane?"

"I don't know, I am sure. What's this? Can you tell a bear track when you see it?"

"Of course I can," answered Don, and the listeners heard him pushing his way through the cane toward the path in which his brother stood. "But I don't call this a bear track," he added, after a moment's pause, during which he was closely examining the footprint his brother pointed out to him. "A barefooted man or boy has been along here, and that track was made not more than ten minutes ago. And, Bert," he continued, in a lower tone, "you were right about that boat after all. Come on, now, and if the thief is here we'll have a look at him."

"Pap," whispered Dan, hurriedly, "they're comin' sure's you're livin'. Le's slip around to the other side of the island, easy like, and steal their boats afore they know what is goin' on."

"We couldn't do it," replied his father, in the same cautious whisper. "They'd be sure to see us. I'll fix 'em when they come nigh enough. I'd like to shoot 'em both, to pay 'em for findin' my hidin' place."

"Don't do that, pap," said Dan, in great alarm. "Here they come, an' - Laws a massy? What's that?"

As Dan uttered these words, a deep, hoarse, growl, so suddenly and fiercely uttered, that it almost made his hair stand on end, sounded close at his side. Don and Bert heard it, and they were as badly frightened as Dan was.

"What was that, Don?" asked Bert, in an excited whisper. "You heard it, didn't you?"

"I should think so," was Don's reply, and the words were followed by the clicking of the locks of his gun.

After that came a long pause. Don and Bert waited for the warning growl to be repeated, and stooping down, tried to peer through the cane in front of them, in the hope of obtaining a view of the animal, which had been disturbed by their approach, while Dan, crouching low in his place of concealment, looked first at his father and then glanced timidly about, as if in momentary expectation of seeing something frightful. He could hardly bring himself to believe that the noise, which so greatly terrified him, had been made by his father, but such was the fact.

If there was a person in the world, Godfrey did not want to meet face to face, that person was Don Gordon; and when he first became aware that the boy was close at hand, and that he was about to explore the island, he was greatly alarmed and utterly at a loss how to avoid him. If Don saw him there, of course he would tell of it, and that would set the officers of the law on his track (no evidence that could be produced was strong enough to convince Godfrey, that he had nothing to fear from the officers of the law) and compel him to look for a new hiding-place. The conversation he overheard between the brothers, regarding the capture of the bear, which had so long held possession of the island, brought a bright idea into his mind, and he acted upon it at the right time, too. It was the only thing that saved him from discovery. Don was not afraid of a man, and if he had known that Godfrey was hidden in the cane a few feet in advance of him, he would have walked straight up to him, and accused him of stealing his boat; but he had no desire to face a wild animal alone and unaided, and he was in no condition to do it, either. We say alone and unaided, because Bert would have been of no assistance to him. Bert was a famous shot with his double-barrel, and no boy in the settlement could show more game, after a day spent among the waterfowl, than he could; but he was too timid and excitable to be of any use to one placed in a situation of danger. Even the sight of a deer dashing through the woods, or the whirr of a flock of quails as they unexpectedly arose from the bushes at his feet, would set him to shaking so violently that he could not shoot.

"What do you suppose it was, Don?" asked Bert, and Godfrey did not fail to notice that his voice trembled when he spoke. "Was it a wild cat or a panther?"

"O, no," replied Don. "One of those animals wouldn't warn us. He'd be down on us before we knew he was about. I wish I had my rifle and the free use of my legs. I'd never leave the island until I had one good pop at him."

A slight rustling in the cane told the listeners that Don was again advancing slowly along the path. Dan was afraid that he had made up his mind to risk a shot with his double-barrel, and so was Godfrey, who uttered another growl, louder and fiercer than the first, and rattled the cane with his hands. That was too much even for Don's courage; and Bert was frightened almost out of his senses.

"Look out, Don! Look out!" he exclaimed. "He is coming!"

"Let him come," replied Don, retreating backward along the path.

"Run! run!" entreated Bert.

"That's quite impossible. I'm doing the best I can now. If he shows himself I'll fill his head full of number six shot."

Godfrey continued to growl and rattle the cane at intervals, but there was no need of it, for Don was quite as anxious to reach his boat and leave the island as Godfrey and Dan were to have him do so. He retreated along the path with all the speed he could command, holding himself ready to make as desperate a fight as he could if circumstances should render it necessary, and presently a rattlin of oars and a splashing in the water told the listeners that he and his brother were pushing off and making their way down the bayou. In order to satisfy himself on this point, Godfrey crawled over the pile of cane, behind which he had been concealed and moved quickly, but noiselessly along the path, closely followed by Dan. On reaching the edge of the cane they looked down the stream and saw the brothers twenty rods away in their boat, Bert tugging at the oars as if his life depended on his exertions. The danger of discovery was over for the present, but how were Dan and his father to leave the island now without swimming? Don had taken his canoe away with him.

"If I could have my way with them two fellers they'd never trouble nobody else," exclaimed Godfrey, shaking his fist at the departing boat. "Whar be I goin' to hide now, I'd like to know?"

"Stay here," replied Dan, "an' if they come back to pester you, growl 'em off 'n the island like you done this time."

"An' git a bullet into me fur my pains?" returned his father. "No, sar. Don'll be up here agin in the mornin', sartin, an' he'll have his rifle with him, too; but I won't be here to stand afore it, kase I've seed him shoot too ofter. He kin jest beat the hind sights off'n you, any day in the week."

"Whoop!" cried Dan, jumping up and knocking his heels together.

"I don't see what bring them two oneasy chaps up here, nohow," said Godfrey, taking no notice of the boy's threatening attitude. "I never knowed them or anybody else to come up the bayou in a small boat afore, 'ceptin' when that bar was killed here. That was an amazin' smart trick of mine, Dannie. Howsomever, we hain't got no more time to talk. I'm goin' to give you five dollars, Dannie, an' I want you to go to the landin' an' spend it fur me. Get me a pair of shoes - number 'levens, you know - an' two pair stockin's, an' spend the heft of the rest fur tobacker. Then when it comes dark, I want you to get that canoe agin, an' bring it up here with the things you buy at the store."

"How am I goin' to git the canoe?"

"Take it an' welcome, like I did."

Dan shrugged his shoulders, and his father, believing from the expression on his face that he was about to refuse to undertake the task, made haste to add: -

"An' when you come, Dannie, I'll tell you how we're goin' to work it to git them hundred and fifty dollars that Dave's goin' to 'arn by trappin' them birds fur that feller up North. I have a right to it, kase I'm his pap: an' when I get it, I'll give you half - that is, if you do right by me while I'm hidin' here. I'll give you half that bar'l, too, when we find it. Then you kin have your circus hoss an' all your other nice things, can't you?" added Godfrey, playfully poking his son in the ribs.

Dan's face relaxed a little, but his father's affected enthusiasm was not as contagious now as it was when the subject of the buried treasure was first brought up for discussion. Godfrey had no intention of renewing his efforts to find the barrel - he could not have been hired to go into that potato-patch after what had happened there - but it was well enough, he thought, to hold it up to Dan as an inducement. Besides, if he could get the boy interested in the matter again, and induce him to prosecute the search, and Dan should, by any accident, stumble upon the barrel, so much the better for himself. The great desire of his life would be attained. He would be rich, and that, too, without work.

"Why can't you steal the canoe yourself?" asked Dan.

"Kase I've got to pack up an' get ready to leave here; that's why. It'll take me from now till the time you come back to get all my traps together."

Dan hurriedly made a mental inventory of the valuables his father possessed and which he had seen in the camp, and the result showed one rifle, one powder-horn and one bullet-pouch. All Godfrey had besides he carried on his back. It certainly would not take him three or four hours to gather these few articles together.

"Pap's mighty 'feared that he'll do something he can make somebody else do fur him," thought the boy. "But he needn't think he's goin' to get me into a furse. I ain't agoin' to steal no canoe fur nobody."

"An' since it's you," added Godfrey, seeing that Dan did not readily fall in with his plans, "I'll give you a dollar of my hard-'arned money for doin' the job."

"Wal, now that sounds like business," exclaimed Dan, brightening up. "Whar's the money, an' how am I goin' to get off'n the island?"

"The money's safe, and I'll bring it to you in a minute," replied Godfrey. "You stay here till I come back. As fur gettin' acrosst the bayou, that's easy done. Thar's plenty of drift wood at the upper end of the island, an' you kin get on a log an' pole yourself over. When you get home, Dannie, make friends with Dave the fust thing you do, an' tell him you was only foolin' when you said you was goin' agin him. Help him every way you kin, an' when he gits the money we'll show our hands."

So saying, Godfrey walked down the path out of sight. After a few minutes' absence, he came back and handed Dan the money of which he had spoken, a five-dollar bill to be expended for himself at the store, and a one-dollar bill to pay Dan for stealing the canoe. When Dan had put them both carefully away in his pocket, he went back to the camp after his rifle, and then followed his father through the cane toward the upper end of the island. They found an abundance of drift wood there, and from it selected two small logs of nearly the same size and length. By fastening these together with green withes, a raft was made, which was sufficiently buoyant to carry Dan in safety to the main land. When it was completed, the boy swung his rifle over his shoulder by a piece of stout twine he happened to have in his pocket, and taking the pole his father handed him, pushed off into the stream.

Poling the raft was harder work than rowing the canoe, and Dan's progress was necessarily slow; but he accomplished the journey at last, and after waving his hand to his father, disappeared in the bushes. He took a straight course for the landing and after a little more than an hour's rapid walking, found himself in Silas Jones's store. He was greatly surprised at something he saw when he got there, and so bewildered by it that he forgot all about the money he had in his pocket, and the stockings, shoes and tobacco of which his father stood so much in need. There was David making the most extravagant purchases, and there was Silas bowing and smiling and acting as politely to him as he ever did to his richest customers. If Dan was astonished at this, he was still more astonished, when David threw down a ten-dollar bill and the grocer pushed it back to him with the remark, that his credit was good for six months. Dan could not imagine how David had managed to obtain possession of so much money, and when he found out, as he did when he and his brother were on their way home, he straightway went to work to think up some plan by which he might get it into his own hands. This problem and a bright idea, which suddenly suggested itself to him, occupied his mind during the walk; and shortly after parting from his brother at General Gordon's barn, Dan hit upon a second idea, which made his usually gloomy face brighten wonderfully while he thought about it.

Dan's first duty was to rectify his mistake of the morning, and make his brother understand that he had repented of the determination he had made to work against him, and that he was going to do all he could to assist him. He tried to do this, as we know, but did not succeed, for to his great surprise and sorrow David announced that he was not going to waste any more time in building traps for Dan to break up, and this led the latter to believe that nothing more was to be done toward catching the quails. He walked slowly around the cabin, after a short interview with his brother, and the first thing he saw on which to vent his rage was Don's pointer, which came frisking out of his kennel and wagging his tail by way of greeting, only to be sent yelping back again by a vicious kick from Dan's foot.

"I'm jest a hundred an' fifty dollars outen pocket an' so is pap," soliloquized Dan, almost ready to cry with vexation when he thought of the magnificent prize which had slipped through his fingers. "A hundred an' fifty dollars! My circus hoss an' fine gun an' straw hat an' shiny boots is all up a holler stump, dog-gone my buttons, an' that thar's jest what's the matter of me. An' what makes it wusser is, I lost 'em by bein' a fule," added Dan, stamping his bare feet furiously upon the ground.

Just then a lively, cheerful whistle sounded from the inside of the cabin where David was busy arranging his purchases. Things were taking a turn for the better with him now, and he whistled for the same reason that a bird sings - because he was happy.

"If I could only think up some way to make that thar mean Dave feel as bad as I do, how quick I'd jump at it! I wish pap was here. He'd tell me how. He's as jolly as a mud-turtle on a dry log on a sunshiny day, Dave is, while I - Whoop!" yelled Dan, jumping up and striking his heels together in his rage. "Howsomever, I'll have them ten dollars afore I take a wink of sleep this blessed night -"

Here Dan stopped and looked steadily at the pointer for a few minutes. Then he slapped his knee with his open hand, thrust both arms up to the elbows in his pockets and walked up and down the yard, smiling and shaking his head as if he were thinking about something that afforded him the greatest satisfaction.

CHAPTER VIII

DOGS IN THE MANGER

David would not have been as happy as he was if he had known all that was going on in the settlement. As it happened, his father and brother were not the only ones he had to fear. These two had an eye on the money he expected to earn by trapping the quails, and for that reason they were not disposed to interfere with him until his work was all done and he had reaped the reward of it; but there were two others who had suddenly made up their minds that it was unsportsmanlike to trap birds and that it should not be done if they could prevent it. They were Lester Brigham and his particular friend and crony - almost the only one he had in the settlement, in fact - Bob Owens.

Bob lived about two miles from General Gordon's, and might have made one of the select little company of fellows with whom Don and Bert delighted to associate, if he had been so inclined. But he was much like Dan Evans in a good many respects, and had been guilty of so many mean actions that he had driven almost all his friends away from him. He rode over to the General's about twice each week, and while he was there he was treated as civilly and kindly as every other visitor was: but the brothers never returned his visits, and would have been much better satisfied if Bob had stayed at home.

These two boys, Lester and Bob, were determined that David should not earn the hundred and fifty dollars if they could help it, and they knew that by annoying him in every possible way, they would annoy Don and Bert, too: and that was really what they wanted to do. What reason had they for wishing to annoy Don and Bert? No good reason. Did you ever see a youth who was popular among his fellows, and who was liked by almost everybody, both old and young, who did not have at least one enemy in some sneaking boy, who would gladly injure him by every means in his power? Lester and Bob were jealous of Don and Bert, that was the secret of the matter; and more than that, they were disappointed applicants for the very contract which Don had secured for David.

Bob regularly borrowed and read the *"Rod and Gun,"* and when his eye fell upon the advertisement calling for fifty dozen live quails, he thought he saw a chance to make a goodly sum of pocket money, and hurried off to lay the matter before his friend Lester, proposing that they should go into partnership and divide the profits. Of course Lester entered heartily into the scheme. He knew nothing about building and setting traps, but Bob did, and when they had discussed the matter and calculated their chances for success, they told each other that in two weeks' time the required number of birds would be on their way up the river. That very day Bob addressed a letter to the advertiser, and as soon as it was sent off he and Lester went to work on the traps.

It is hardly necessary to say that they lived in a fever of excitement and suspense after that, and anxiously awaited an answer from the gentleman who wanted the quails. The mail was brought in by the carrier from the county seat, on Wednesday and Friday afternoons, and Bob and Lester made it a point to be on hand when the letters were distributed. One Wednesday, about two weeks after the letter applying for the order was mailed, Bob went down to the post-office alone, and the first person he met there was Bert Gordon. They leaned against the counter and talked while the mail was being put into the boxes, and when the pigeon-hole was opened, the postmaster handed each of them a good-sized bundle of letters and papers, which they began to stow away in their pockets, glancing hastily at the addresses as they did so. It happened that each of them found a letter in his bundle, which attracted his attention, and, as if moved by a common impulse, they walked toward opposite ends of the counter to read them.

The letter Bert found was addressed to Don; but he was pretty certain he could tell where it came from, and knowing that his brother wouldn't care - there were no secrets between them, now - he opened and read it. He was entirely satisfied with its contents, but the other boy was not so well satisfied with the contents of his. When Bert picked up his riding-whip and turned to leave the store, he saw Bob leaning against the counter, mechanically folding his letter, while his eyes were fastened upon the floor, at which he was scowling savagely.

"What's the matter?" asked Bert. "No bad news, I hope."

"Well, it is bad news," replied Bob, so snappishly, that Bert was sorry that he had spoken to him at all. "You see, I found an advertisement in one of your father's papers, asking for live quails. I wrote to the man that I could furnish them, and I have just received an answer from him, stating that he has already sent the order to another party, and one who lives in my immediate neighborhood. What's the matter with you?" exclaimed Bob, as Bert broke out into a cheery laugh.

"When did you write to him?" asked Bert.

"On the very day I borrowed the paper."

"Well, Don was just three days ahead of you. I've got the order in my pocket."

"What do you and Don want to go into the trapping business for?" asked Bob, with ill-concealed disgust. "You don't need the money."

"Neither do you," replied Bert.

"Yes, I do. I intended to buy a new shot-gun with it. I am almost the only decent fellow in the settlement who doesn't own a breech-loader. I have racked my brain for months, to think up some way to earn money enough to get one, and when I am just about to accomplish my object, you and Don have to jump up and rob me of the chance. The man tells me that he would be glad to give me the contract, if he hadn't given it to you. I've a good notion to slap you over."

"It isn't for us," replied Bert. "It is for Dave Evans; and I think you will acknowledge that he needs the money if anybody does."

"Dave Evans!" sneered Bob.

"Yes; and he needs clothes and food more than you need a new shot-gun."

"I guess I know what I want and how much I want it," retorted Bob. "I'm to be shoved aside to give place to that lazy ragamuffin, am I? If I don't make you wish that you had kept your nose out of my business, I'm a Dutchman."

Bert did not wait to hear all of this speech. Seeing that Bob was getting angrier every minute, and that his rage was likely to get the better of him, he drew on his gloves, mounted his pony and set out for home. Bob followed a quarter of a mile or so in his rear, and once or twice he whipped up his horse and closed in on Bert as if he had made up his mind to carry out his threat of slapping him over. But every time he did so a sturdy, broad-shouldered figure, with a face that looked wonderfully like Don Gordon's, seemed to come between him and the unconscious object of his pursuit, and then Bob would rein in his horse and let Bert get farther ahead of him. Presently Bob came to a road running at right angles with the one he was following, and there he stopped, for he saw Lester Brigham approaching at a full gallop. The latter was by his side in a few seconds, and his first question was: -

"Been to the post-office?"

"I have, and there's the letter on which I built so many hopes," replied Bob, handing out the document which he had crumpled into a little round ball. "We were too late. The order has been given to that meddlesome fellow, Don."

Lester looked first at his companion, then at Bert, who was now almost out of sight, and began to gather up his reins.

"You'd better not do it, unless you want to feel the weight of his brother's arm," said Bob, who seemed to read the thoughts that were passing through Lester's mind. "I gave him a good going-over, and told him I had a notion to knock him down."

"Why didn't you do it?" exclaimed Lester. "I'd have backed you against Don or anybody else."

"Haw! haw!" laughed Bob. "I shall want *good* backing before I willingly raise a row in that quarter, I tell you."

"What do you mean by that?" demanded Lester.

"O, I was just joking, of course. But what's to be done about this business? Don got the contract for Dave Evans, and I want to know if we are to be kicked out of the way to make room for him."

Lester did not reply at once. He did not feel very highly flattered by the low estimate Bob seemed to put upon him as a "backer" in case of trouble with Don Gordon, and while he was trying to make up his mind whether he ought to let it pass or get sulky over it, he was unfolding and smoothing out the letter he held in his hand. When he had made himself master of its contents, he said: -

"You come over and stay with me to-night, and we'll put our heads together and see what we can make of this. I must go down to the store now, and I'll meet you here in half an hour.

That will give you time enough to go home and speak to your folks."

Bob spent the night at Lester's house, and it was during the long conversation they had before they went to sleep, that they made up their minds that it was a mean piece of business to trap quails, and that nobody but a miserable pot-hunter would do it. They adopted the dog-in-the-manger policy at once. If they could not trap the birds, nobody should; and that was about all they could decide on just then.

The next morning after breakfast they mounted their horses and rode in company, until they came to the lane that led to Bob's home and there they parted, Lester directing his course down the main road toward the cabin in which David Evans lived. He met David in the road, as we know, and laid down the law to him in pretty strong language; but strange enough the latter could not be coaxed or frightened into promising that he would give up his chance of earning a hundred and fifty dollars.

Lester was in a towering passion when he rode away after his conversation with David. Lashing his horse into a run, he turned into the first road he came to, and after a two-mile gallop, drew rein in front of the double log-house in which Bob Owens lived. There was an empty wagon-shed on the opposite side of the road, and there he found Bob, standing with his hands in his pockets, and gazing ruefully at the pile of traps upon which he and Lester had worked so industriously, and which he had hoped would bring them in a nice little sum of spending money.

"Well, did you see him?" asked Bob, as his friend rode up to the shed and swung himself out of the saddle.

"I did," was the reply, "and he was as defiant as you please. He was downright insolent."

"These white trash are as impudent as the niggers," said Bob, "and no one who has the least respect for himself will have anything to do with them. I used to think that Don Gordon was something of an aristocrat, but now I know better."

"I wish I had given him a good cowhiding," continued Lester, who did not think it worth while to state that he had been on the point of attempting that very thing, but had thought better of it when he saw how resolutely David stood his ground. "But never mind. We'll get even with him. We'll touch his pocket, and that will hurt him worse than a whipping. It will hurt the Gordons, too."

"Then he wouldn't promise to give up the idea of catching them quails? I am sorry, for if we could only frighten him off the track, we would write to that man up North telling him that the party with whom he made his contract wasn't able to fill it, but we could catch all the birds he wants in two weeks."

"That's a good idea - a splendid idea!" exclaimed Lester; "and perhaps we'll do it any how, if the plan I have thought of doesn't prove successful."

Lester then went on to repeat the conversation he had had with David, as nearly as he could recall it, and wound up by saying: -

"I told him that we were going to start a Sportsman's Club among the fellows, and that after we got fairly going, our first hard work should be to break up this practice of trapping birds. Of course that wasn't true - I just happened to think of it while I was talking to him - but why can't we make it true? If all the boys will join in with us, I'd like to see him do any trapping this winter."

"But who can we get to go in with us?"

"We'll ask Don and Bert the first thing."

"Nary time," exclaimed Bob, quickly. "If they are the sort

you're going to get to join your club, you may just count me out. I don't like them."

"You like them just as well as I do; but we have an object to gain, and we mustn't allow our personal feelings to stand in our way."

"Do you suppose Don would join such a club after getting Dave the job?"

"Perhaps he would. He likes to be first in everything, doesn't he?"

"I should say so," replied Bob, in great disgust. "I never saw a fellow try to shove himself ahead as that Don Gordon does."

"Well, we'll flatter him by offering to make him President of the club; and we'll promise to make Bert Vice or Secretary."

"I'll not vote for either of them."

"Yes, you will. We want to get them on our side; for if they promise to go in with us every boy in the settlement will do the same."

"That's what makes me so mad every time I think of those Gordons," exclaimed Bob, spitefully throwing down a stick which he had been cutting with his knife. "Every fellow about here, except you and me, is ready to hang on to their coat tails and do just what they do. One would think by the way they act that they belonged to some royal family. They don't notice me at all. They've had a crowd of boys in that shooting-box of theirs every spring and fall since I can remember, and I have never had an invitation to go there yet. They take along a nigger to cook for them, and have a high old time shooting over their decoys; but the first thing they know they'll find that shanty missing some fine morning. I'll set fire to it."

"Don't say that out loud," said Lester, quickly, at the same time extending his hand to his companion, as if to show that what he had said met his own views exactly. "Don't so much as hint it to a living person. We'll give them a chance to make friends with us if they want to, and if they don't, let them take the consequences. But we can talk about that some other time. What do you say to getting up a Sportsman's Club?"

Bob did not know what to say, for he had never heard of such a thing until he became acquainted with Lester. The latter explained the objects of such organizations as well as he could, and after some debate they crossed over to the house, intending to go into Bob's room and draw up a constitution for the government of the proposed society. On the way Bob suddenly thought of something.

"You and I want to earn this money, don't we?" said he. "That's what we're working for, isn't it? Well, now, if we put a stop to trapping, how are we going to do it?"

"This is the way we're going to do it: we'll drive Dave Evans off the track first. When that is done, we'll tell that man up North that we are the only one's here who can fill his order. Then we'll go quietly to work and catch our birds, saying nothing to nobody about it, and when we have trapped all we want, we'll ship them off."

"But somebody will see us when we are putting them on the boat."

"No matter for that. The mischief will be done, and we'll see how Don and Dave will help themselves. We can afford to be indifferent to them when we have seventy-five dollars apiece in our pockets, can't we?"

"Lester, you're a brick!" exclaimed Bob. "I never could have thought up such a plot. I'll have my gun after all."

"Of course you will."

"And what will become of the club?"

"We don't care what becomes of it. Having served our purpose, it can go to smash and welcome. Now will you vote for Don and Bert?"

"I'll be only too glad to get the chance. But you'll have to manage the thing, Lester."

"I'll do that. All I ask of you is to talk the matter up among the boys, that is, if Don and Bert agree to join us, and put in your vote when the time comes."

The two friends spent the best part of the day in Bob's room, drawing up the constitution that was to govern their society. Lester, who did all the writing, had never seen a document of the kind, and having nothing to guide him he made rather poor work of it. He had read a few extracts from game laws, and remembered that Greek and Latin names were used therein. He could recall some of these names, and he put them in as they occurred to him, and talked about them so glibly, and appeared to be so thoroughly posted in natural history that Bob was greatly astonished. Of course there was a clause in the instrument prohibiting pot-hunting and the snaring of birds, and that was as strong as language could make it. The work being done at last to the satisfaction of both the boys, Lester mounted his horse and galloped away in the direction of Don Gordon's home.

CHAPTER IX

NATURAL HISTORY

Lester Brigham was not at all intimate with Don and Bert. The brothers, as in duty bound, called upon him when he first arrived in the settlement, and a few days afterward Lester rode over and took dinner with them; and that was the last of their visiting. The boys could see nothing to admire in one another. Don and Bert were a little too "high-toned;" in other words, they were young gentlemen, and such fellows did not suit Lester, who preferred to associate with Bob Owens and a few others like him. Lester had been a leader among his city schoolmates, and he expected to occupy the same position among the boys about Rochdale; but before he had been many weeks in the settlement he found that there were some fellows there who knew just as much as he did, who rode horses and wore clothes as good as his own, and who had some very decided opinions and were in the habit of thinking for themselves. They wouldn't "cotton" to him even if he was from the city, and so Lester made friends with those whom he regarded as his inferiors in every way.

Lester was not at all pleased with the task he had set himself on this particular day. He never felt easy in Don's presence and Bert's, and nothing but the hope of compelling David to give up his contract and thus leave the way clear for Bob and himself, would have induced him to call upon them. He rode slowly in order to postpone the interview as long as he could, but the General's barn was reached at last, and the hostler, who

Harry Castlemon

came forward to take his nag, told him that Don and Bert had just gone into the house. The latter opened the door in response to his knock, and Lester knew by the way he looked at him that he was very much surprised to see him. But he welcomed him very cordially, and conducted him into the library, where Don was lying upon the sofa.

"That night in the potato cellar was a serious matter for you, wasn't it?" said the visitor, after the greeting was over and he had seated himself in the chair which Bert placed in front of the fire. "Haven't you been able to take any exercise at all yet?"

"O, yes; I've been out all day. I've had almost too much exercise, and that is what puts me here on the sofa."

"We've had some excitement, too," added Bert.

"Yes. We went up the bayou to see if the ducks had begun to come in any yet, and we found a bear on Bruin's Island."

"Did you shoot him?"

"No. He gave us notice to clear out and we were only too glad to do so. Such growls *I* never heard before."

"One's nerves do shake a little under such circumstances, that is, if he is not accustomed to shooting large game," said Lester, loftily. "You ought to have had me there. Perhaps I'll go up some day and pay my respects to him."

Don, who thought this a splendid opportunity to test Lester's courage, was on the very point of telling him that he and Bert were going up there the next day to see if they could find the animal, and that they would be glad to have his assistance; but on second thought he concluded that he would say nothing about it. He expected to have some sport as well as some excitement during the trip, and he didn't want his day's enjoyment spoiled by any such fellow as Lester Brigham.

"I came over to see you two boys on business," continued the visitor, drawing an official envelope from his pocket. "We talk of getting up a Sportsman's Club here in the settlement: will you join it?"

"Who are talking of getting it up, and what is the object of it?" asked Don.

"All the boys are talking of it. One object is to bring the young sportsmen of the neighborhood into more intimate relations, and another is to protect the game. Perhaps I can give you no better idea of the proposed organization than by reading this constitution, which will be acted upon by the club at its first meeting."

As Lester said this he looked from one to the other of the brothers, and receiving a nod from each which signified that they were ready to listen, he drew out the document of which he had spoken, and proceeded to read it in his best style. He glanced at his auditors occasionally while he was reading the paper, and when he came to a certain paragraph, the one upon which he and Bob had expended the most time and thought, he told himself that he had certainly made an impression, for Bert looked bewildered and Don straightened up, drew a note-book from his pocket and began making entries therein with a lead-pencil. The paragraph read as follows:

"The great object of the club being to put down pot-hunters and poachers, and stop the practice, which is so common, of trapping game and shipping it out of the country, it is hereby

"*Resolved*, that on and after the date of the adoption of this constitution, it shall be unlawful for any person to take by trapping, at any season of the year, or on any lands, whether private in their own occupation, public or waste, any of the game animals and birds hereinafter described, to wit: pheasant (*T. Scolopax*); partridge (*Picus Imperialis*); rabbit (*Ortyx Virgiana*); and red deer (*Canis Lupus*). The penalty for disobedience shall be a fine of ten dollars for the first offence, twenty for the second, thirty for the third, and so on; the fines to be sued and recovered before any justice of the peace in the county, and to be divided in equal parts between the informer and the poor; and in default of payment the offender shall be imprisoned for ten days in the county jail."

When the document was finished, Don asked him to read this clause over again. He complied with the request, and as he folded the paper very deliberately waited for his auditors to say a word of commendation; but as they didn't do it, he said it himself.

"Now, I drew up that instrument, and I think it is just about right," said he, complacently. "It is nothing but the truth, if I do say it myself, that there is not another fellow in the settlement who could have done it. Of course it will be open to amendments, but I don't see how or where it could be improved. It covers all the ground, doesn't it?'

"It covers a good deal, and especially the article you read twice," replied Don. "But I can't join such an organization as that. I'm a pot-hunter myself. I never went hunting yet, without I intended to shoot something for the table."

"But you are not a poacher."

"I don't know about that. I hunt in every field and piece of woods I find, no matter who owns them."

"Perhaps I had better change that," said Lester, after thinking a moment, "and say market-shooters instead of pot-hunters."

"There are no such things as market-shooters in the county."

"But there are market-trappers," said Lester. "There are persons here, who are catching quails and shipping them out of the state."

"Yes, there is one who thinks of going into the business, and I got him the job. It wouldn't look very well for me to turn around now and tell him that he must not do it."

"You could say to him that you have had reason to change your mind lately, and that you know it isn't right to do such things."

"But I haven't changed my mind."

"You ought to. The first thing you know there will be no birds for you and me to shoot."

"I'll risk that. You may trap two hundred dozen if you want to, and send them out of the county, and when you have done it, I will go out any morning with my pointer and shoot birds enough for breakfast. I'll leave more in the fields, too, than you can bag in six months," added Don, and Bert saw the point he was trying to make, if Lester did not. "Besides, what right have I to tell Dave what he shall do and what he shall not do? He'd laugh at me."

"Well, he wouldn't do it more than once. A few days in the calaboose would bring him to his senses."

"Who would put him there?"

"The club would."

"Where's the club's authority for such a proceeding?"

Lester lifted the constitution and tapped it with his forefinger by way of reply.

"I think I had better have nothing to do with it," said Don, who could scarcely refrain from laughing outright.

"We intend to make you our president," said Lester.

"I am obliged to you," replied Don, but still he did not take any more interest in the Sportsman's Club than he had done before. He did not snap up the bait thus thrown out, as Lester hoped he would. He was not to be bought, even by the promise of office. Lester saw that, and arose to take his leave.

"Well, think it over," said he. "Sleep on it for a few nights, and if at any time you decide to go in with us, just let me know. Good evening!"

"I'll do so," answered Don. "Good evening!"

Lester bowed himself out of the room and Bert accompanied him to the door. The first question the latter asked when he came back was: -

"Is there a beast or a bird in the world whose Latin name is canis-lupus?"

Don threw himself back upon the sofa and laughed until the room rang again. "Is there a beast or a bird in the world whose English name is dog-wolf?" he asked, as soon as he could speak. "I did give Lester credit for a little common sense and a little knowledge, but I declare he possesses neither. It beats the world how he has got things mixed. Just listen to this," added Don, consulting his note-book. "He speaks of a pheasant and calls it *T. Scolopax*. Now *Scolopax* is a snipe. He probably meant ruffed grouse, and should have called it *Tetrao Umbellus*. He speaks of a partridge when he means quail, or more properly Bob White, there being no quails on this side the Atlantic -"

"Why do people call them quails then?" asked Bert.

"The name was given to them by our forefathers, because they resembled the European quail. There is no pheasant in America either; but our grouse looked like one, and so they gave it that name, Lester calls a quail *Pious Imperialis*. Now that's an imperial woodpecker - that big black fellow with a red topknot that we sometimes see when we are hunting. He used to be called cock-of-the-woods, but the name was twisted around until it became woodcock, and some people believe that he is the gamey little bird we so much delight to shoot and eat. But they belong to different orders, one being a climber and the other a wader. Lester speaks of a rabbit, not knowing that there is no such thing as a wild rabbit in our country, and calls it *Ortyx Virgiana*, when he should have called it *Lepus Virginianus*, the name he uses being the one by which our quail is known to ornithologists. A deer, which he calls a dog-wolf, is *Cervus Virginianus*. O, he's a naturalist as well as a sportsman," shouted Don, as he laid back upon the sofa and laughed until his sides ached.

"Then he didn't get one of the names right?"

"Not a single one. After all, his ignorance on these points is not so astonishing, for everybody is liable to make mistakes; but that any boy living in this day and age should imagine that, by simply getting up a club and adopting a constitution, he could imprison or fine another boy because he didn't do just to suit him, is too ridiculous to be believed. That particular paragraph was probably copied after some old game law Lester read years ago; but he ought to know that before a sportsman's club, or any other organization, can have authority to prosecute persons for trapping birds and sending them away, there must first be a law passed prohibiting such trapping and sending away; and there's no such law in this state. It doesn't seem possible that he could have been in earnest."

But Lester was in earnest for all that - so very much in earnest that he was willing to run a great risk in order to punish Don for refusing to join his society. Of course he was angry. He and Bob had felt sure of obtaining the contract, had laid many plans for the spending of the money after it was earned, and it was very provoking to find that their scheme had been defeated, and that they were to be pushed aside for the sake of such a fellow as David Evans. Lester was sorry now that he had not given David a good thrashing when he met him in the road that morning, and told himself that he would do it the very next time he put eyes on him and risk the consequences. The thought had scarcely passed through his mind when the opportunity was presented. He met David coming along the road in company with his brother Dan. David did not seem to remember that any sharp words had passed between Lester and himself, for he looked as cheerful and smiling as usual, and, following the custom of the country, bowed to the horseman as he rode past. Lester did not return the bow, and neither did he dismount to give David the promised thrashing. He was afraid to attempt it; but, coward-like, he had to take vengeance upon something, and so he hit his horse a savage cut with his riding-whip.

"Dave can afford to be polite and good-natured," thought Lester, as he went flying down the road. "He is rejoicing over his success and my failure; but if he only knew it, this thing isn't settled yet. I'll write to that man to-night, telling him, that the parties to whom he gave the contract can't catch the birds, and then Bob and I will go to work and make it true. If we don't earn that money, nobody shall. As for those stuck-up Gordons - I'll show them how I'll get even with them."

The spirited animal on which he was mounted made short work of the two miles that lay between Don's home and Bob's, and in a few minutes Lester dismounted in front of the wagon-shed, where his crony was waiting for him.

"I've had no luck at all," said he, in reply to Bob's inquiring look. "I might as well have stayed at home. Don says he can't join a club of this kind, because, having got David the job of trapping the quails, he can't go back on him. He says he's a poacher and pot-hunter himself; and what surprised me was, he did not seem to be at all ashamed of it."

"Of course he wasn't ashamed," said Bob. "He thinks that everything he and his pale-faced brother do is just right. Did he say anything about what passed between Bert and myself at the post-office?"

"Not a word."

"I was afraid he would," said Bob, drawing a long breath of relief, "for he knows that you and I are friends."

Yes, Don knew that, but there were two good reasons why he had not spoken to Lester about Bob's threat of slapping Bert over. In the first place, he was not aware that Bob had made any such threat. Bert was one of the few boys we have met, who did not believe in telling everything he knew. Do you know such a boy among your companions? If you do, you know one whom nobody is afraid to trust. Bert wanted to live in peace, and thought it a good plan to quell disturbances, instead of helping them along. He knew that if he told his brother what had happened in the post-office, there would be a fight, the very first time Don and Bob met, and Bert didn't believe in fighting. But even if Don had known all about it, he would not have said anything to Lester. He would have waited until he met Bob, and then he would have used some pretty strong arguments, and driven them home by the aid of his fist. How much trouble might be avoided, if there were a few more boys like Bert Gordon in the world!

"I am not sorry I went down there," continued Lester, "for I had the satisfaction of showing those conceited fellows that there are some boys in the settlement besides themselves who know a thing or two. I read the constitution to them, and it would have made you laugh to see them open their eyes. Bert was so astonished that he couldn't say a word, and Don never took his gaze off my face while I was reading. When I got through he asked me to read that clause with the Latin and Greek in it over again, so that he could copy the names in his note-book. He'll learn them by heart, and use them some time in conversation and so get the reputation of being a very smart and a very learned boy. If he does it in your presence, I want you to let folks know that he is showing off on the strength of *my* brains. I don't suppose the ignoramus ever knew before -"

"Well, who cares whether he did or not?" exclaimed Bob,

impatiently. "That's a matter that doesn't interest me. Is Dave Evans going to make that hundred and fifty dollars and cheat me out of a new shot-gun? That's what I want to know!"

"Of course he isn't," replied Lester. "We can't stop him by the aid of the Sportsman's Club, and so we will stop him ourselves without the aid of anybody. Let him go to work and set his traps, and we'll see how many birds he will take out of them. We'll rob every one we can find and keep the quail ourselves. In that way we may be able to make up the fifty dozen without setting any of our own traps. We'll write to that man, as you suggested, and when Dave finds he can't catch any birds, he'll get discouraged and leave us a clear field. But first I want to touch up Don and Bert Gordon a little to pay them for the way they treated me this evening. That shooting-box shall be laid in ashes this very night. I expected an invitation to shoot there last spring, but I didn't get it, and now I am determined that they shall never ask anybody there. What do you say?"

"I say, I'm your man," replied Bob.

And so the thing was settled. Lester put his horse in the barn, went in to supper, which was announced in a few minutes (Bob found opportunity before he sat down to the table to purloin a box of matches, which he put carefully away in his pocket), and when the meal was over, the two boys went back to the wagon-shed, where they sat and talked until it began to grow dark. Then Bob brought a couple of paddles out of the corner of the wagon-shed, handed one to his companion, and the two walked slowly down the road. When they were out of sight of the house they climbed the fence, and directed their course across the fields toward the head of the lake. Then they quickened their pace. They had much to do, and they wanted to finish their work and return to the house before their absence was discovered.

Half an hour's rapid walking brought them to the road just below General Gordon's barn. The next thing was to make their way along the foot of the garden until they reached the jetty, and that was an undertaking that was not wholly free from danger. Don Gordon's hounds were noted watch-dogs, and any prowlers they discovered were pretty certain to be severely treated. But there was no flinching on the part of the two boys. Bob led the way almost on his hands and knees, stopping now and then to listen, and finally brought his companion to the place where the boats were moored. There was only one of them available, however, for the canoe, which they had intended to take, was secured to a tree by a heavy padlock.

"Did you ever hear of such luck?" whispered Bob.

"Couldn't we paddle the other up there?" asked Lester, feeling of the chain with which the sail-boat was fastened to the wharf, to make sure that it was not locked.

"O, yes; but why is this canoe locked up? That's what bothers me. Perhaps Don suspects something and is on the watch."

"Who cares if he is?" exclaimed Lester. "I've come too far to back out now. I wouldn't do it if Don and all his friends stood in my way."

"All right. If you are not afraid, I am not. Be careful when you cast off that chain. You know that sound travels a long way on a still night like this."

Lester was careful, and the boat was pushed off and got under way so noiselessly that a person standing on the bank would not have known that there was anything going on. Bob, who knew just where the shooting-box was located, sat in the stern and did the steering, at the same time assisting Lester in paddling. The heavy boat moved easily through the water, and before another half hour had passed they were at their journey's end.

"Hold up now," whispered Bob, "and let's make sure that everything is all right before we touch the shore."

Lester drew in his paddle and listened. He heard a whistling in the air, as a solitary duck flew swiftly up the lake, and that was the only sound that broke the stillness. The trees on the shore loomed up darkly against the sky, and presented the appearance of a solid wall of ebony. Lester could not see anything that looked like a shooting-box, but Bob knew it was there, and when he had listened long enough to satisfy himself that there was nobody in it or about it, he brought the bow of the boat around and paddled toward the shore.

"Which way is it from here?" asked Lester, when the two had disembarked. "I can't see anything."

"Hold fast to my coat-tail," replied Bob, "and I'll show it to you in a minute."

Lester being thus taken in tow was safely conducted up the bank. Presently he heard a door unlatched and opened, a match was struck and he found himself inside the shooting-box. He could scarcely have been more surprised if he had found himself inside a little palace. The shooting-box was not a shanty, as he expected to find it, but a conveniently-arranged and neatly-constructed house. He borrowed a few matches of Bob and proceeded to take a thorough survey of it. "Don must have spent a good deal of time in fixing this up," said he.

"He certainly has," replied Bob, "and he handles tools like a born carpenter, too. I suppose this is a nice place to get away to when the fellows are here shooting over their decoys. Joe Packard says so, at any rate. They have mattresses and bed clothes in the bunks, a carpet and rugs on the floor, camp chairs and stools enough for the whole party, and they sit here of evenings and crack hickory-nuts and tell stories and have boss times."

"It's almost a pity to break up their fun."

"It's a greater pity that Don should take money out of our pockets and put it into those of that beggar, Dave Evans," answered Bob, spitefully.

"That's so," said Lester, who grew angry every time he thought of it. "Set her agoing!"

That was a matter of no difficulty. There was an abundance of dry fuel and kindling wood in the little closet under the chimney, and some of the latter was quickly whittled into shavings by the aid of Bob's pocket knife, Lester standing by and burning matches to light him at his work. More kindling wood was placed upon the shavings, dry stove wood was piled upon the top of this, then the slats in the bunks, the table and every other movable thing in the cabin that would burn was thrown on, and Bob took a match in his hand and extended another to his companion.

"You light one side and I'll light the other," said he. "Then you can't say I did it, and I can't say you did it!"

The matches blazed up on opposite sides at the same instant. The flames made rapid progress, and by the time the boys had closed the door and got into the boat, they were roaring and crackling at a great rate. They quickly shoved off and laid out all their strength on the paddles, but before they could reach the jetty the flames burst through the roof of the shooting-box, and the lake was lighted up for a quarter of a mile around. But no one saw it, and Lester and his companion put the boat back where they found it, made their way across the road into the fields, without alarming the hounds, and started for home on a keen run, no one being the wiser for what they had done.

CHAPTER X

A BEAR HUNT

"I'll jest do it, an' it's the luckiest thing in the world that I thought of it. That will make me wuth - " here he stopped and counted his fingers - "twenty-two dollars and two bits, anyhow. Then my clothes, an' stockings, an' shoes, an' all the powder an' lead I want this winter, won't cost me nothing; so I shall be rich fur all that thar mean Dave is workin' so hard agin me."

It was Dan Evans who talked thus to himself, and he was standing behind the cabin, with his hands in his pockets, and looking at Don's pointer, just as he was the last time we saw him. He was so very much delighted with certain plans he had determined upon that that he did not dare meet his brother again just then, for fear that the expression of joy and triumph which he knew his face wore would attract David's notice and put him on his guard. So he remained in the rear of the cabin with his thoughts for company, until his mother came home. The dress David had purchased for her, and which he had placed in the most conspicuous position he could find, was the first thing that attracted her attention as she entered the door. Dan heard her exclamation of joyful surprise, and listened with all his ears in the hope of overhearing some of the conversation that passed between her and David; but it was carried on in a low tone of voice, and Dan was no wiser when it was concluded than he was before. He knew, however, by the ejaculations that now and then fell from his mother's lips that

David was telling her something which greatly interested her, and Dan would have given almost anything to know what it was. He heard his mother laugh a little occasionally, and that brought the scowl back to his face again. He could not bear to know that any one about that house was happy.

When supper was over, and David had done the chores and assisted in clearing away the dishes, he and his mother seated themselves in front of the fireplace and prepared to pass the evening in conversation, as they always did, while Dan threw himself upon the "shake-down" on which he and his brother slept, and in a few minutes began snoring lustily. He was not asleep, however. His ears were open, and so were his eyes the most of the time. He saw everything that was done and heard all that passed between his mother and David, but not a word did he hear that interested him. David had already given his mother a history of the events of the day. She knew what his plans were and approved them.

When nine o'clock came David took possession of the other half of the "shake-down" and prepared to go to sleep. He deposited his clothes at the head of the bed, as usual, and Dan, through his half-closed eyes, saw that he threw them down in a careless sort of way, as though there was nothing of value in them.

"But he can't fool me so easy," thought Dan. "Not by no means. Thar's ten dollars somewhar in them thar dry goods, unless he give 'em to the ole woman when she fust come hum, an' they'll be mine afore mornin'. He wouldn't go snacks with me, like a feller had oughter do, an' now I'll have 'em all!"

In an hour from that time everybody in the cabin appeared to be asleep. Mrs. Evans certainly was and David seemed to be, for he lay with his eyes closed, and breathed long and heavily. Dan took a good look at him - the blazing fire on the hearth made the cabin almost as light as day - and then reaching out his hand drew David's clothes toward him. He searched all the pockets carefully, but there was nothing in them except a pocket-knife with two broken blades, and that was not what Dan was looking for. Muttering something under his breath Dan turned all the pockets inside out and then felt of the lining of the coat; but as nothing rewarded his search he tossed the clothes back upon the floor, and cautiously slipped his hand under his brother's pillow. As he did so David suddenly raised himself upright in bed, and seizing the pillow, lifted it from its place.

"If you want to look under there, why don't you say so?" he asked.

Almost any other boy would have been overcome with shame and mortification, but Dan was not easily abashed, and although he felt a little crestfallen, his face did not show it.

"It isn't there you see, don't you?" said David.

"What isn't thar?" growled Dan.

"Why, the ten-dollar bill you saw me have at the landing. It isn't in my clothes either, or anywhere about the house."

"I wasn't lookin' fur it," returned Dan.

"I'll tell you where it is, if you want to know," continued David. "It is safe in Don Gordon's pocket-book, and you can't get it out of there. I told you that you'd never have another chance to steal any of my money, and I think you will believe it now. Good-night, and pleasant dreams to you; that is, if you can sleep after such a performance."

Dan could sleep, and he did, too, after he got over his rage, but his night's rest did not seem to refresh him much, for he was cross and sullen the next morning, and ate his breakfast without saying a word to anybody. David was as bright as a lark; and after he had assisted his mother in her household duties, he took down his rusty old single-barrel from the pegs over the fireplace, slung on his powder-horn and shot-pouch, and when his mother was ready to go, he accompanied her down the road toward General Gordon's, leaving Dan sitting on the bench, moody and thoughtful.

"They don't take no more notice of me nor if I was a yaller dog or a crooked stick," growled Dan, when he found himself alone. "I'll pay 'em fur it by kickin' up a wusser row nor pap done 'bout that thar bar'l, an' I shan't be long a doin' of it nuther!"

Mrs. Evans and David separated at the forks of the road, the former directing her course toward the house of the neighbor by whom she was employed, and David hurrying on toward General Gordon's. When he reached the head of the lake he heard a loud shout; and looking in the direction from which it came, he saw Don and Bert standing on the wharf beckoning to him. David ran across the garden to join the brothers, and found that they were all ready to start on the hunt they had planned the day before. A well-filled basket, which David knew contained a substantial lunch, stood on the wharf, and near it lay the General's heavy double-barrel gun, which Bert had borrowed for the occasion, knowing that it would throw buck-shot with more force than his light bird gun. Bert was unfastening the canoe, and Don stood close by, with his trusty rifle in one hand and an axe in the other. Two other axes lay near the lunch basket, and a couple of Don's best hounds stood as close to the edge of the wharf as they could get, wagging their tails vigorously and whining with impatience.

These hounds were large and powerful animals, and their courage had been tested in more than one desperate bear fight. If they had been with their master when he visited the island the day before, something disagreeable might have happened. Godfrey Evans could not have driven them away by imitating the growl of a wild animal. They welcomed the newcomer with their bugle-like notes, and were answered by a chorus of angry yelps from the rest of the pack, which had been shut up in the barn and were to be left behind.

"Now, I call this rather a formidable expedition," said Don, as David came up. "If that bear is there to-day I wouldn't take a dollar for my chance of shooting him. One bullet and three loads of buckshot will be more than he can carry away with him. Here are the axes to build the trap with, if we don't find him on the island; there's a bag of corn for bait, an auger to bore the holes and the pins with which to fasten the logs together. Bert and I worked in the shop last night until ten o'clock, making those pins. I think we have everything we wan't, so we'll be off."

The canoe having been hauled alongside the wharf, and the articles which Don had enumerated being packed away in it, the hounds jumped in and curled themselves up in the bow, David took his place at the oars and the brothers found comfortable seats in the stern. Altogether it was a heavy load the little boat had to carry, and she was so deep in the water that her gunwales were scarcely three inches above the surface; but there were never any heavy seas to be encountered in that little lake, and so there was no danger to be apprehended.

David sent the canoe rapidly along, and presently it entered the bayou that led to Bruin's Island. As it approached Godfrey Evans's cabin Dan arose from the bench on which he was seated in front of the door, and ran hastily around the corner of the building. He did not mean that Don and Bert should see him again, even at a distance, if he could help it. He remained concealed until the canoe was out of sight, and then came back to his bench again.

While on the way up the bayou the young hunters stopped once, long enough to pick up a brace of ducks which Bert killed out of a flock that arose from the water just in advance of them, and at the end of an hour came within sight of the leaning sycamore which pointed out the position of Bruin's Island. There was no one to be seen, but that was no proof that the island was deserted. There was some one there whom the three boys did not expect to see or hear of very soon, and that was Godfrey Evans. He was waiting for Dan to come with the canoe and the tobacco and other articles he had been instructed to purchase at the store. He had watched for him until long after midnight, then retreated to his bed of leaves under the lean-to for a short nap, and at the first peep of day he was again at his post behind the sycamore. To his great relief he saw the boat coming at last, but his joy was of short duration, for a second look showed him that Dan was not in it.

The canoe came nearer to the island with every stroke of the oars, and presently one of Don's hounds started to his feet, snuffed the air eagerly for a moment and uttered a deep-toned bay. Godfrey ducked his head on the instant and crawled swiftly away from the sycamore on his hands and knees. He was careful to keep the tree between himself and those in the boat until he reached the cane, and then he arose to his feet and worked his way toward his camp with all possible haste.

"Them two oneasy chaps has come back agin, just as I thought they would," said he to himself, "and our Dave's with 'em. Don's got his rifle now and his dogs, too, so't thar ain't no use tryin' to scare him this time. I must hunt a new hidin'-place now."

Godfrey stopped in his camp just long enough to seize his rifle and ammunition; after which he plunged into the cane again and ran toward the head of the island. The muddy beach was thickly covered with drift-wood, and behind a convenient pile of branches and logs Godfrey crouched down and waited to see what was going to happen.

The actions of Don's hounds made the young hunters almost as nervous as they made Godfrey Evans. David stopped tugging at the oars and looked over his shoulder; Bert caught up his father's double-barrel and hastily loaded it with two cartridges containing buckshot; while Don, after bringing the canoe broadside to the island, dropped the paddle with which he was steering, and picked up his rifle.

"He's there yet," said Bert. "The hounds have scented him already."

"It looks like it," replied Don. "Well, we came here to find him, and if he drives us away to-day he'll have to fight to do it. Dave, you'd better load up - Bert has plenty of loose buckshot in his pocket - and mind you now, fellows, don't get excited and shoot the dogs. I'd rather let the bear go than have one of them hurt."

While David was loading his single-barrel - his hands trembled a little, and it took him longer than usual to do it - Don and Bert sat with their guns across their knees, closely watching the island, while the hounds stood in the bow snuffing the air. They caught some taint upon the breeze, that was evident, for the long hair on the back of their necks stood erect and now and then they growled savagely.

When David had driven home a good-sized charge of buckshot and placed a cap upon his gun, he leaned the weapon against the thwart upon which he was sitting and picked up the oars. Don dropped his paddle into the water, and the canoe moved around the foot of the island and along the beach, until it reached a point opposite the place where Bert had found the path the day before. Then it was turned toward the bank, and the moment the bow grounded, the hounds sprang out. The boys followed with all haste, and Bert, as he stepped ashore, drew the canoe half way out of the water, so that the current could not carry her down the stream.

"Now, we'll send the dogs in to drive him out," said Don, "and if they can push him fast enough to make him take to a tree, he's our bear; but if he takes to the water and swims to the mainland, we shall lose him. We don't care for that, however. He'll be sure to come back, and when he does he'll find a trap waiting for him. We'll see as much sport in catching him alive as we would in shooting him. Hunt 'em up, there!" he added, waving his hand along the path.

The hounds, baying fierce and loud at every jump, went tearing through the cane, followed by the boys, who moved in single file, Don leading the way. A very few minutes sufficed to bring them to the cleared spot in which Godfrey's camp was located, and there they found the hounds running about showing every sign of anger and excitement.

"They're on a warm trail," said Don, looking first into each corner of the cleared space and then up into the trees over his head. "The game has just left here. This is somebody's old camp, and the bear has taken possession of it. No doubt he slept in that shanty. Hunt 'em up, there!"

The hounds followed Godfrey's trail through the camp, and diving into the cane on the opposite side were quickly out of sight. The boys followed, and presently stood panting and almost breathless beside the drift-wood where the hounds were running about close to the water's edge, now and then looking toward the opposite shore and baying loudly. But Godfrey was safely out of their reach. Seizing the opportunity when the hunters and dogs were hidden from view in the cane, he stepped into the water and struck out for the mainland. He had hardly time to climb the bank and conceal himself in the bushes before Don's hounds were running about on the very spot where he had been hidden but a few minutes before. Why was it that the hounds followed his trail as they would have followed that of a bear or deer? Simply because they scented him before they reached the island, and because Godfrey took so much pains to keep out of their way. Had he stood out in plain view while the boat was approaching, the hounds would have paid no attention to him.

"Well, he's gone," said Bert, and the deep sigh that escaped his lips as he uttered the words would have led one to believe that he was glad of it, "and now comes the hard work. It's an all-day's job to build that trap."

"It would be if we had to cut down the trees and trim off the branches," replied David; "but there is some timber in this drift-wood that will answer our purpose as well as any we could get ourselves. Where are you going to build the trap, Don?"

"In there where his den is would be the best place, wouldn't it? Now let's go after the axes; and while you and Bert are cutting the logs, I'll unload the boat and open a road through the cane, so that we can haul our timber in without any difficulty."

The work being thus divided rapid progress was made. By the time Don had unloaded the boat and cut a path leading from Godfrey's camp to the upper end of the island, Bert and David had selected and notched all the logs that were needed for the trap. Then a stout rope, which Don had been thoughtful enough to put into the boat, was brought into requisition, and the work of hauling in the logs began. As fast as they were placed in position, Don fastened them down with the pins he and his brother had made the night before, and when lunch time came, a neat log cabin about six feet square was standing in front of Godfrey's lean-to. With a little "chinking" and the addition of a door and perhaps a window, it would have made a much more comfortable place of abode than the miserable bark structure which Godfrey had so long occupied.

Their hard work had given the boys glorious appetites, and they did full justice to the good things Mrs. Gordon had put up for them. Don said their lunch might have been much improved by the addition of one of the ducks Bert had shot that morning, but their time was much too precious to be wasted in cooking. The hardest part of their task was yet to be done, and that was to build a movable roof for their cabin. Don, who had received explicit instructions from his father the night before, superintended this work, and by the middle of the afternoon the trap was completed and set, ready for the bear's reception.

It looked, as we have said, like a little log cabin with a flat roof. One end of the roof rested on the rear wall of the trap, while the other was raised in the air, leaving an opening sufficiently large to admit of the entrance of any bear that was likely to come that way. The roof was held in this position by a stout lever, which rested across the limb of a convenient tree. A rope led from the other end of the lever, down through a hole in the roof, to the trigger, to which the bait - an ear of corn - was attached. The bear was expected to crawl through the opening and seize the ear of corn; and in so doing, he would spring the trigger, release the lever and the roof would fall down and fasten him in the pen. When all the finishing touches had been put on, the boys leaned on their axes and admired their work.

CHAPTER XI

TRAPPING QUAILS

"Now, I call that a pretty good job for a first attempt," said Don; "and considering the work we have had to do, it hasn't taken us a great while either. I wish I dare crawl in there and set it off, just to be sure that it will work all right."

"But that wouldn't be a very bright proceeding," replied Bert. "We could never get you out. You would be as securely confined as you were when you were tied up in the potato-cellar."

Don was well aware of that fact. The roof was made of logs as heavy as they could manage with their united strength, and there were other logs placed upon it in such a position that when the roof fell, their weight would assist in holding it down. All these precautions were necessary, for a bear can exert tremendous strength if he once makes up his mind to do it; and David had repeatedly declared that if they should chance to capture an animal as large as the one that had been killed on that very island years before, the pen would not prove half strong enough to hold him. But it was quite strong enough to hold Don if he got into it, and the only way his companions could have released him would have been by cutting the roof in pieces with their axes.

The work was all done now, and the boys were ready to start for home. While Bert and David were gathering up the tools and stowing them away in the canoe, Don scattered a few ears of corn around, so that the bear would be sure to find them the next time he visited the island, and threw a dozen or so more into the trap close about the trigger. The rest of the corn he hung up out of reach on a sapling which he knew was too small for the bear to climb.

Assisted by the current the canoe made good time down the bayou. Bert and David lay back in the stern-sheets and said they were tired, while Don, who was seated at the oars, declared that his day's work had relieved his stiff joints, and that he began to feel like himself again. He was fresh enough to assist in building another trap without an hour's rest; and in order to work off a little of his surplus energy, he thought when he reached home he would take a turn through the fields in company with his pointer, and see if he could bag quails enough for his next morning's breakfast. Bert said he would go with him, for he wanted to see the pointer work.

In about three quarters of an hour the canoe entered the lake and drew up to the bank in front of Godfrey's cabin. David sprang out, and after placing his gun upon the bench in front of the door, went behind the building to unchain the pointer. He was gone a long time - so long that Don and Bert, who were sitting in the canoe waiting for him, began to grow impatient - and when he came back he did not bring the pointer with him. He brought instead a chain and a collar. His face told the brothers that he had made a most unwelcome discovery.

"Where's the dog?" asked Bert.

"I don't know," answered David, looking up and down the road. "He must have slipped the collar over his head and gone off; but I never knew him to do it before."

"Well, you needn't look so sober about it," said Don. "He isn't far away. I'll warrant I can bring him back."

Don set up a whistle that could have been heard for half a mile. Indeed it was heard and recognised at a greater distance than that. An answering yelp came from the direction of his father's house, but it was not given by the dog Don wanted to see just then. It was uttered by one of the hounds which had been shut up in the barn when Don went away that morning, and afterward released by the hostler. The others answered in chorus, and half a dozen fleet animals were seen coming down the road at the top of their speed. But the pointer was not with them.

"It's likely we shall find him at the house," said Bert, who wanted to say something encouraging for David's benefit.

"I don't doubt it," returned Don. "If he's there, Dave, we'll take a short hunt with him and bring him down in the morning."

"If you don't care I'll go up with you," said David, "It would be a great relief to me to know that he is safe."

"All right. Jump aboard."

David got into the canoe again and Don pulled up the lake toward the wharf. When they reached it the boat was made fast to the tree again, and the three boys started for the house. Don at once began making inquiries concerning his pointer, but no one had seen him, and his loud and continued whistling brought only the hounds, which snuffed at the guns and yelped and jumped about as if trying to make their master understand that they were there, and ready for anything he might want them to do.

"Never mind," said Don, who did not seem to feel half as bad as David did; "dogs of his breed never stray far away, and he'll be at your house or ours before morning, you may depend upon it. Good-by now, and don't forget to be on hand at an early hour. We must set to work upon those traps without any more delay."

David reluctantly turned his face toward home, and Don and Bert went into the house. "I didn't tell him just what I think about the matter, for he feels badly enough already," said Don, when he and his brother were in their room, dressing for supper. "There's an awful thief about here, and it wouldn't surprise me at all to know that the pointer has gone where our canoe went."

"Do you know that that thought has been in my mind all the while?" returned Bert. "Who is the thief?"

"I give it up. If he lives about here he's foolish to steal my dog, for he never can use him in hunting. There isn't a man or boy in the settlement but would recognise him the moment he saw him."

"Perhaps he was stolen in the hope that a reward would be offered for his return," suggested Bert.

"Well, there's something in that. But after all," added Don, a few minutes later, "there isn't so much in it, for how could the thief return the dog without making himself known? Still I hope it is so - that is, if the dog was stolen - for rather than lose him, I'll give ten dollars to anybody who will bring him back to me, and ask no questions. If I have to do that it will ruin me, for it will take my last cent."

The ringing of the supper bell put a stop to their conversation for the time being, but it was resumed as soon as the family were gathered about the table. Various explanations were offered for the pointer's absence, and when that matter had been talked over, the events of the day were brought up for discussion. Bert acted as spokesman, and when he told how the hounds had driven the bear from his den and forced him to swim the bayou, Don was surprised to see that his father smiled as if he did not quite believe it. "It's the truth, every word of it," said Don, almost indignantly.

"O, I don't doubt that you found something on the island and drove it off," replied the General, "but I don't think it was a bear."

"What was it?" asked Don.

"It was something you will not be likely to catch in your trap. It was Godfrey Evans."

Don dropped his knife and fork, and settled back in his chair. "We saw tracks in the mud that did not look to me like bear tracks, that's a fact," said he. "If that was Godfrey, he's the one who stole our canoe."

"Then we have had all our trouble for nothing," said Bert.

"Perhaps not," replied his father. "The island has been much frequented by bears ever since I can remember, and it may be that your labor will be rewarded in a day or two. It might be well for you to watch your trap at any rate. If you should happen to catch a young bear, that you could bring home alive, Silas Jones would give you twenty dollars for it. That would be a big addition to David's little capital, for of course you wouldn't want any of the money."

"Of course not. All we want is the fun of catching the bear."

Don and Bert were up the next morning before the sun, as they always were, and as soon as they were dressed, they went out to the shop and found David there busy with his traps. He knew where the key was kept, under the door-step, and at the first peep of day he had let himself in and gone to work. Of course the first questions that were asked and answered were in regard to the missing pointer, but no one had seen or heard anything of him. David seemed to take the loss very much to heart. The animal was a valuable one, and he felt that he was in some degree responsible for his safe-keeping.

Three pairs of willing hands made light work, and by two o'clock in the afternoon a dozen traps were completed and ready for setting. The boys then stopped long enough to take a hasty lunch, which they ate in the shop, in order to save time, and after that one of the mules was hitched to a wagon and brought before the door. The traps, a basket containing the "figure fours," with which they were to be set, a bag of corn for bait, an axe, with which to clear away the underbrush, and a spade to dig the trenches, having been packed away in the vehicle, the boys got in and drove off. They directed their course along the fence, which ran around the plantation, and wherever they found a clump of bushes or a little thicket of briers and cane, there they stopped long enough to set one of their traps.

The traps were made of slats split from oak boards, and were a little less than four feet square and a little more than a foot in height. In the top was a slide covering a hole large enough to admit one's arm, and it was through this hole that the captured birds were to be taken out. The undergrowth was first cut away with the axe and the trap put down in the clear space, a narrow board being placed under two sides of it, to give it a solid foundation. A trench just large enough to admit a single quail was dug under each of these boards, one end of the trench being on the outside of the trap and the other on the inside. A small ear of corn was tied firmly to the trigger, the trap set with the "figure four," a few kernels were scattered about in the immediate neighborhood, and the trap was ready for the first flock of quails that might come that way. When they came, they would, of course, find the corn, and while they were eating it they would be sure to find the trap. One or more of them would go in and spring it by pecking at the ear that was tied to the trigger, and the others, no matter if there were a hundred in the flock, would all go in to him through the trenches before spoken of. After they had eaten the corn, they would look *up* instead of down for a way of escape, and, although the trenches at which they came in were still open to them, they would not know enough to make use of them. If the trap was once sprung, the capture of the entire flock was certain, provided those outside were not frightened away before they had time to go in to their imprisoned companions.

In two hours' time the traps had all been set and the boys were at home again. They had done a good day's work, but they wanted to do a better; so as soon as the mule was unharnessed and the wagon put under the shed where it belonged, they set to work in the shop again, and before dark a large coop, which would just fit into the wagon box, was completed. This was to be used to bring home the captured quails. After that one of the unoccupied negro cabins was selected to confine the birds in until the required number had been trapped. It received a thorough sweeping, the floor was covered with clean sand, and the broken window was boarded up so that the captives could not escape. When this was done David started for home, and Don and Bert went into the house to get ready for supper.

The next day was spent much as the preceding one had been spent. At eleven o'clock seven more traps were ready for the field. Then the mule and wagon were brought into use again, and the new traps were distributed along the fence. When the boys came back they took time to eat lunch, after which the coop was put into the wagon, and they set out to visit the traps they had set the day before.

"There's nothing here," said Bert, as he drew rein in front of the thicket in which the first trap was located. He could not see the trap, but his ears told him all he wanted to know. If there had been any quails in it they would have uttered their notes of alarm as soon as they heard the wagon coming.

"No, there's nothing here!" said Don, after listening a moment. "I'll scatter a little more corn about and make sure that the trap is all right."

He got out of the wagon as he spoke, and while he was working his way into the thicket he flushed a blue-jay, which flew into a tree close by and scolded him with all its might. Don shied a stick at it and kept on to the trap. It was down, and there was something in it which fluttered its wings against the bars and made the most frantic efforts to escape. Don knew it was not a quail, so he did not stop to see what it was.

He threw back the slide, thrust his hand into the opening and when he clutched the bird received a severe bite from it. "I have half a mind to wring your little neck for you," thought Don, as he brought the fluttering captive, a beautiful red-bird, into view. "Not because you have bitten me, but because you will make it your business to come here and spring this trap every day. Red-birds and blue-jays are perfect nuisances when a fellow is trapping, and I wouldn't blame Dave for shooting every one he sees."

But Don did not injure the bird. He was a sportsman, and never made war on game of this sort. He tossed the captive into the air and it flew away out of sight.

Having set the trap again and scattered a little more corn about to replace that which had been picked up by the birds, Don went back to the wagon and Bert drove on down the field. They found the second trap thrown, and the marks of little teeth on the ear of corn that was tied to the trigger showed that a ground squirrel had been at work. The third trap was also sprung, and the shrill, piping notes of alarm which came to their ears when Bert stopped the wagon, told them that they had made their first capture. Jumping quickly out of the wagon the boys made their way into the bushes, and when they came within sight of the trap they found that it was so full that the little prisoners had scarcely room to turn about. "Here's the first instalment of your hundred and fifty dollars, Dave," cried Don. "We've got more than a dozen, I know!"

Having stopped up the ends of the trenches so that the quails could not escape, Don thrust his arm through the opening in the top of the trap and began passing out the birds to his brother and David, who carried them to the wagon and put them into the coop. He counted them as he took them out, and found that there were nearer two dozen than one, twenty being the exact number. One, however, escaped from Bert, who, through fear of injuring it, handled it too tenderly.

"Never mind," said Don, when his brother told him of the

loss. "He'll go off and join some other flock, so we are bound to catch him anyhow. I call this a good beginning, don't you, Dave? It looks now as though you were going to earn your money in spite of Lester and Dan."

After re-setting the trap the boys got into the wagon and drove on. They found some of their traps just as they had left them; a few had been thrown by ground squirrels or red-birds; and from the others they took enough quails to make their day's catch amount to a little over four dozen. These were all safely transferred to the cabin, the mule was unharnessed and the young trappers, greatly encouraged by their success, replenished the fire in the shop, for the day was raw and chilly, and went to work to build more traps.

CHAPTER XII

WHERE THE POINTER WAS

"Yes, sar, I'm goin' to raise a furse here now, an' I won't be long about it, nuther. They think I don't amount to nothin' in this yere house, but I'll show 'em that I do. Pap bein' away, I had oughter be the man of the family, an' that leetle Dave shan't crowd me outen the place, nuther. When he comes back to-night his eyes'll stick out so't a feller could hang his hat onto 'em. You hear me?"

This was the way Dan Evans talked to himself, as he sat on the bench in front of the door, gazing after his mother and David, as they walked down the road toward General Gordon's. He was greatly enraged over his failure to steal his brother's ten dollars, and really thought David had been guilty of a mean piece of business in putting his money where it would be safe.

"He hain't went off with that thar shootin'-iron on his shoulder fur nothin'," thought Dan. "He's goin' huntin' with them Gordon fellers, and he'll have a nice time an' get somethin' good to eat, while I must go without my dinner, dog-gone it, kase thar hain't nobody here to cook it fur me. They don't take half so much notice of me as they would if I was a pinter dog!"

Dan sat on the bench for half an hour or more, now and then looking down the road as if he were waiting for something, and all the while his mind was occupied with such thoughts as these. At last the sight of Don Gordon's canoe, which suddenly appeared in the lake, brought him to his feet and sent him behind the cabin in great haste. It did more. It recalled to him the fact that his father had told him to steal that same canoe and bring it to Bruin's Island, together with several necessary articles that were to be purchased at Silas Jones's store. Dan had not once thought of this since he saw David at the landing with ten dollars in his hand, and heard the grocer tell him that his credit was good for six months; but he thought of it the moment he saw the canoe with the hounds curled up in the bow. His eyes were sharp enough to see that Don carried his rifle in his hands, and that a heavy shot-gun, which Dan knew belonged to General Gordon, leaned over Bert's shoulder. Godfrey's prediction was about to be fulfilled. Don was going back to the island to shoot the bear which had frightened him and his brother the day before. The thought made Dan almost frantic. He jumped up and knocked his heels together, slapped his hands, dashed his hat upon the ground and made other demonstrations indicative of a very perturbed state of mind.

"Pap's in fur it now, an' so am I," said he, in an excited whisper. "He'll get his jacket wet swimmin' the bayou to get away from them fellers, if they give him the chance, an' I'll get mine dusted with a hickory, kase I didn't fetch that canoe up thar. I jest wish I knowed what to do."

Dan, almost ready to cry with vexation and alarm, watched the canoe until it turned into the bayou and passed out of his sight, and then went back to the bench and sat down to think about this new difficulty in which he found himself, and to find a way out of it if he could. His father would be compelled to hunt up a new hiding-place now - there was no way to prevent that - and in order to leave the island he would probably be forced to swim the bayou, for he would have no time to build a raft. That would, of course, make him angry, and he never could breathe easily again until he had taken satisfaction out of somebody. That somebody Dan knew was certain to be himself, unless -

"I'll fix him," thought the boy, his face clearing up, as a bright idea came into his mind. "I'll take him the pinter. I was goin' to hide him in the woods somewhar, but pap kin take keer on him as well as not. Don'll pay a dollar or two to get him back, an' I'll give the ole man half. But fust, I must go down to the landin' an' buy them shoes an' tobacker; an' while I'm thar, I'll jest say a good word to Silas fur myself. I'm a nobody about this yere house, am I? Dave wouldn't give me them ten dollars to keep fur him, an' now I'll take somethin' outen his pocket without sayin' a word to him."

Dan shook his head in a very wise and knowing manner, and went into the house after his rifle. He did not take it because he expected to find any game while he was on the way to the landing, but because he had fallen into the habit of carrying it with him everywhere he went and felt lonely without it.

Knowing that Don and Bert were not at home, Dan did not go around through the fields to avoid the General's barn, as he usually did, but boldly followed the road. There were a few idle men hanging about the store, as there almost always were, but none of them appeared to be doing any trading, and the grocer was ready to attend to Dan's wants at once. The boy bought the articles his father wanted, and having pocketed his change, cleared his throat, preparatory to saying a good word for himself.

"Mr. Jones, if you please, sar, Dave done sent me down here this mornin' to ax you would you give me somethin' fur myself, if you please, sar - some shoes an' sich like."

"Certainly," replied the grocer, readily, and Dan was surprised to see that he held out his hand as if he expected to receive something.

"I hain't got no money," said Dan.

"That makes no difference. I don't want any money from David."

"Then I'll take a pair of them amazin' fine lookin' shoes of your'n - number nines, please, sar."

"All right. Hand out the order."

"Sar!" exclaimed Dan, opening his eyes.

"Why, if David doesn't come here himself and tell me to give you the things, he must send a written order."

"Dave, he done told me to git 'em," faltered Dan.

"I don't doubt it; but in order to have things straight, you go home and get an order for such things as you want and I'll give them to you."

Dan gathered the articles which he had purchased for his father under one arm, took his rifle under the other, backed slowly away from the counter and went out of the store. He wasn't quite so smart as he thought he was. His shoes and stockings, and the ammunition for his rifle, which he thought he was going to get for nothing, were likely to cost him something after all. It was an easy matter to cheat confiding fellows like Don and Bert, who were much more familiar with Greek than they were with the way business was conducted, but it was not so easy to deceive a man like Silas Jones. Dan was surprised and disappointed, and of course as angry as he could be. He walked rapidly along the road with his bundles, under his arm and his rifle on his shoulder, and it was not until he reached home and had sunned himself for a few minutes on the bench in front of the door, that he cooled down so that he could think the matter over. But he could think to no purpose even then; and after resting a few minutes longer, he arose and went into the cabin.

He walked straight to the "shake-down" which he and his brother occupied, and drew from under the head of it a piece of rope he had placed there the night before. With this in his hand he came out again, and after looking up and down the road, to make sure that there was no one in sight, he went around the building to the kennel where Don's pointer was confined. The animal came out to meet him, and Dan did not send him back with a kick, as he usually did. He took off his collar, and having tied the rope about his neck, buckled the collar again and threw it on the ground, hoping in this way to give David the impression that his charge had liberated himself. He then led the dog to the high rail fence which surrounded the lot, assisted him to climb over it, and left him there in the bushes, while he returned to the bench after his rifle and bundles. These secured, he climbed the fence himself, picked up the rope and hurried into the woods, the pointer trotting along contentedly by his side.

Dan thought he knew just where to go to find his father. The latter would, of course, be on the lookout for his son, and it was reasonable to suppose that he would remain somewhere in the vicinity of the island; so Dan followed the course of the bayou, taking care to keep so far away from it that he would not be discovered by any one who might chance to be passing in a boat, and when he had approached close enough to the island to hear the voices of the young hunters and the sound of their axes, he tied the pointer to a tree, deposited his bundles on the ground near by, and with his rifle for a companion crept through the bushes to see what they were doing.

There was no one in sight when he first reached the bank of the bayou, but in a few minutes Bert and David came out of the cane with a rope in their hands. There were several logs scattered about the beach, and David made the rope fast to one of them and he and Bert dragged it into the cane. While Dan was wondering what they were going to do with the log a twig snapped near him, and he turned quickly to find his father almost within reach of him.

"Halloo, pap!" said Dan, jumping to his feet and backing into the bushes.

"Whar's the tobacker?" demanded Godfrey, in a subdued tone

of voice.

"I've got it. You ain't mad, be you, pap?"

"I ain't so scandalous mad now, but if I could have got my fingers into your collar about the time I was a shiverin' in my wet clothes, I'd a played 'Far'well to the Star Spangled Banner' on your back with a good hickory, I bet you!"

"'Kase if you be mad 'tain't my fault," continued Dan. "I tried my level best to steal the canoe, but couldn't do it. It was locked up tighter'n a brick. I tried to get ten dollars fur you too, pap, but I couldn't do that nuther; so I brung Don Gordon's pinter along. Swum the bayou, I reckon, didn't you?"

"I didn't walk acrosst, did I? In course I swum it."

"Your clothes ain't wet!"

"No, 'kase I went back in the woods an' built a fire an' dried 'em. Le's go back thar now, so't we kin talk. We don't want them fellers to hear us."

"What be they doin' over thar, anyhow?" asked Dan.

"They're buildin' a bar trap, looks like. They'll be sartin to ketch one too, 'kase thar's a bar comes thar a'most every night. If I had a boat they wouldn't get much good of him arter they do ketch him."

Dan handed his rifle to his father and went back after the pointer and his bundles; and when he came up again Godfrey led the way toward his temporary camp. He was gloomy and sullen, and there was an expression on his face which Dan did not like to see there, for it made him fear that a storm was brewing. But after they had been a few minutes in the camp, and Godfrey had filled his pipe and smoked a whiff or two, the scowl faded away and Dan began to breathe easier.

"I've put you in the way to make a dollar, pap," said he, as soon as the soothing effects of the tobacco began to be perceptible. "If you'll take that pinter an' keep him till I call fur him, I'll give you half of what Don pays me to get him back."

"I seed you bringin' the dog an' I knowed what you was up to," replied his father. "But Don don't get him back fur no dollar, I tell you. That animile is wuth fifty dollars anyhow, an' if Don wants him agin he'll have to plank down five dollars."

"Whew!" whistled Dan. "We're gettin' rich, ain't we? Now, pap, thar's your shoes an' stockin's, an' thar's the change Silas give me. You kin put it with what you've got left of your twenty dollars, an' when - O, laws!"

Dan jumped to his feet, opened his mouth and eyes and looked at his father in the greatest astonishment. Something he had said seemed to produce a wonderful effect upon Godfrey. His pipe dropped from his lips, the color all left his face and after sitting silent and motionless for a moment, he gave utterance to a loud yell, sprang to his feet and strode about the camp as if he were almost beside himself.

"What's the matter of you, pap?" Dan ventured to inquire, as soon as he could find his tongue.

"I hain't got no money at all no more!" Godfrey almost shouted. "That's what's the matter of me. It's over thar on the island whar them fellers is!"

"No!" gasped Dan.

"But I say, yes, it is too!" exclaimed Godfrey. "You see," he added, controlling himself with a great effort, "when I fust seed them fellers comin' up the bayou the sun was kinder shinin' on the water, an' it blinded me so't I thought it was you. I was jest goin' to speak, when I seed thar was three fellers in the boat; an' afore I could ax myself what that meant, one of the hounds that Don had with him set up a yelp. I knowed that meant business, an' it skeared me so't I didn't think of nothin' only how to get off'n that thar island without bein' diskivered. I got off all right, but I left my money in that thar holler log, an' I never thought of it till this blessed minute."

"Mebbe they won't find it," said Dan.

"Wal, that's a comfortin' thought," returned his father, sighing heavily, as he picked up his pipe, "but luck's agin me. It allers is. Other folks can get along smooth an' easy, but I can toil an' slave an' slave an' toil till - jest look at me," added Godfrey, rising to his feet again and turning slowly about, so that Dan could have a fair view of him. "Ain't this a purty fix fur a man to be in who owned niggers an' cotton, by the acre only a little while ago? That's jest what makes me 'spise them Gordons."

"An' that's what makes me 'spise that Dave of our'n," exclaimed Dan. "He's gettin' richer every day. He's got ten dollars in greenback money now, an' I done heard Silas Jones tell him that his credit was good at the store for six months."

Godfrey opened his eyes when he heard this, and so interested was he in the story Dan had to tell that he forgot his troubles for the time being. He seated himself again, and while he was refilling his pipe Dan gave him a history of what had happened at the store, and told how David had come by the ten dollars. He also described the manner in which he had tried to obtain possession of it, and told how he had failed in his attempt to induce Silas to give him a pair of shoes on the strength of David's credit. This led to a long discussion between the father and son, during which various plans were laid and one or two things determined upon which will probably be revealed in due time. Dan paid strict attention to all his father said, but he was glad when the interview was over. Godfrey was almost beside himself with fury. Having been unfortunate himself he was enraged to learn that anybody else was prosperous; and when he heard of David's good luck he looked and acted so savagely that Dan began to fear for his own personal safety. He started for home as soon as he could find an excuse for so doing, and it was not until he was out of sight and hearing of his father's camp that he began to breathe easily.

Dan did not go directly home. He was in no hurry to meet his brother, for he was afraid the latter might have something to say to him about the pointer. He roamed through the woods, and having shot a few squirrels, built a fire and roasted and ate them. He stayed in his camp until the sun went down and it began to grow dark, and then shouldered his rifle and reluctantly turned his face toward the cabin. He did not find his brother there, but he came in shortly afterward, and then Dan found that he had been borrowing trouble, for David never said a word to him about the pointer. He told his mother of the loss, and of course she sympathized with him, and offered every explanation except the right one. The thief opened his eyes and looked surprised while they were talking, but neither of them paid any attention to him; and Dan, muttering angrily to himself that he was nothing more than a crooked stick about that house any way, undressed and went to bed.

Dan passed the next day in his usual idle and shiftless manner. He saw David go up to General Gordon's, and would have been glad to know what sort of work he was doing up there, and how much he was to receive for it. He did not find out that day, but he did the next, and the discovery made him feel like a new boy.

Growing tired of staying by himself, Dan thought he would go down to the landing, hoping that he would find a shooting-match going on there, or that a steamer would come in, bringing a stranger or two for him to stare at. The weather was raw and chilly, too, and Dan's bare feet were blue with the cold. He must have a pair of shoes and stockings; and since he couldn't get them in any other way, a portion of the money he had hidden in that hollow log in the woods must be brought into use. Dan took out the necessary amount, and groaned when he looked at the small sum he had left.

As soon as the sun had warmed the air a little, Dan shouldered his rifle and set out. He did not follow the road, as he did before, for that would take him past the General's barn, and Don and Bert were at home now. He went around through the fields; and it was while he was sitting on a log near General Gordon's fence, watching the only squirrel he had seen since leaving home, that he accidentally learned what it was that took David over to Don's house so regularly every morning, and kept him there all day. He first heard the creaking of wheels and the sound of voices, and they came from the General's field, which was not more than twenty feet distant, and which was concealed from his view by the thick bushes that lined the fence. Dan recognised the voices, and his first impulse was to jump up and take to his heels. His next was to stay where he was until the wagon passed by, and this he did; for he was in an excellent hiding-place and no one could have found him without taking pains to look for him.

The wagon came nearer, the voices grew louder, and presently Dan heard the shrill notes of a quail directly in front of him and just on the other side of the fence. He paid no attention to the sound until the wagon was brought to a stand-still in front of the thicket, and somebody, after working his way into the bushes, called out in a cheery voice:

"Here's the first instalment of your hundred and fifty dollars, David!"

These words made Dan so excited that he almost betrayed his presence by letting his rifle fall out of his hands. He cautiously raised himself to a standing position on the log, and looking through the tops of the bushes, listened intently to catch every word that was said.

CHAPTER XIII

TEN DOLLARS REWARD

When the quails had been taken out of the trap and put into the coop, the wagon drove on, and Dan sat down on his log to think about what he had just heard, and to wait until the coast was clear, so that he could resume his walk toward the landing. He had learned two things. One was that his brother had not given up the idea of trapping the quails, as he had supposed, and the other was that there was somebody besides himself whom David had reason to fear.

"Looks now as though you were goin' to 'arn your money in spite of Dan and Lester," thought the listener, recalling the last words he had heard Don utter. "That must be that Brigham boy up to that big white house. What's he got to say 'bout it, I'd like to know? I'll jest keep an eye on him. He don't want to let me ketch him foolin' round them traps, 'kase I'll make him think war times has come back sure enough. Now that I've got another chance to 'arn a share in them hundred and fifty dollars, nobody shan't take it away from me."

Dan was as good as his word. He kept a sharp watch over David's interests, and perhaps we shall see that he was the means of defeating a certain plan, which, if it had been carried into execution, would have worked a great injury to the boy trapper.

The wagon having passed on out of hearing, Dan shouldered

his rifle and started toward the landing. While he was skulking through the woods at the lower end of the field, he stopped in a fence corner long enough to see David and his two friends transfer another good-sized catch from one of the traps to the coop in the wagon. The sight encouraged him greatly. If David's good luck would only continue for just one week, the fifty dozen birds would certainly be captured, and Dan would stand a chance of making a small fortune. It was not so very small either in his estimation. His share would be seventy-five dollars - his father had told him so - and that would make a larger pile of greenbacks than Dan had ever seen at one time in his life. With it he was sure he could buy a new gun as fine as the one Don Gordon owned (he would not have believed it if any one had told him that that little breech-loader cost a hundred and twenty-five dollars in gold), a jointed fish-pole, and some good clothes to wear to church; and when he had purchased all these nice things, he hoped to have enough left to buy a circus-horse like Don's, and perhaps a sail-boat also. Godfrey, for reasons of his own, had held out these grand ideas to him during one of their interviews, and Dan, being unable to figure the matter out for himself, believed all his father told him.

Having seen the second catch put into the coop, Dan started toward the landing again. It was mail day, and consequently there was a larger number of loafers about the post-office than there usually was. Among them were Lester Brigham and Bob Owens, who seemed to be very much interested in something that was fastened to the bulletin-board in the store. Having nothing better to do just then Dan walked up behind them, and looking over their shoulders spelled out with much difficulty the following -

"NOTICE.

"*Ten Dollars Reward.*

"Strayed or stolen, my black-and-white pointer, *Dandy.* I will pay the above reward for his safe return, and ask no questions; or I will give *Five Dollars* for any information that will lead to his recovery.

"DONALD GORDON."

"I am glad he has lost him, and I hope he will never see him again," said Bob, spitefully. "If I knew where he was, I wouldn't tell him for five times five dollars."

"What does he want him back for, anyhow?" said Lester. "Don is assisting in shipping quails out of the country, and the first thing he knows the dog will be of no use to him."

Dan did not waste five minutes in loafing about the store after that. Here was something he had been waiting for ever since he stole the pointer. The owner had offered a heavy reward for his safe return – it was twice as much as Godfrey said they ought to have - and the next thing to be settled was, how to obtain the money, without facing Don Gordon. This was a question over which Dan had often bothered his few brains, but without finding any way of answering it. Something must be determined upon now, however, for there was a nice little sum of money at stake.

Dan made all haste to do his trading, and taking his stockings and shoes under his arm, set out for home, avoiding the road, as he always did when Don and Bert were about, and skulking around through the woods and fields. When he reached the cabin, he seated himself upon the bench beside the door, and there he remained building air-castles until four o'clock in the afternoon. Then he began to bestir himself, and David, who came home that night before his mother did, was surprised to find a roaring fire on the hearth, a pile of wood large enough to last all the evening beside it, and in a pan upon the table a half a dozen squirrels, dressed and ready for the frying-pan.

"What in the world is up now?" thought David. "Dan's got an axe to grind, for he never does such things, unless he intends to make something by it."

"Halloo, Davy!" exclaimed Dan, cheerfully. "I thought mebbe you'd be cold when you come hum, so I built up a fire to warm you. Jest look at them thar squirrels, will you? Every one on 'em was shot through the head. Can you beat that?"

"No," answered David. "It can't be beaten."

"If we had a few quail now, we'd have a bully supper, wouldn't we?" continued Dan. "You don't seem to shoot no more quail lately, do you, Davy?"

"O, I can't hunt them without a dog to tell me where they are."

"Hain't you never heard nothin' from that pinter pup at all?"

"Not a word."

"I'm sorry. I wish I knowed whar he was, so't I could fetch him hack. I'm scandalous mad at myself fur takin' that money from you an' Don, an' if I had ten dollars I'd give 'em back to-night; but I hain't got 'em, an' so I'm goin' to try an' find his dog fur him."

"He'll be very glad to get him," said David, who knew very well that his brother had some other reason for taking this sudden interest in the pointer.

"I want to act decent now, like a gentleman had oughter act," Dan went on; "an' if I do what I can fur Don, do you reckon he'll call it squar'?"

"I don't know. You must talk to him about that."

"But I ain't agoin' to face him 'till I know how he feels towards me, I bet you. I don't know whar the dog is, more'n the man in the moon; but I'm kinder scentin' round, when I hain't got no work to do, an' if I should happen to find him, would you take him to Don fur me?"

"Of course I would, and be very glad to do it."

"Then I'll do what I kin, an' if I do say it myself, I kin find him if anybody kin. I kin afford to spend all my time lookin' fur him, kase I was down to the landin' to-day, an' I seed a notice stuck up thar sayin' that Don'll give ten dollars fur him an' ax no questions. What's the matter of you?" demanded Dan, as David turned quickly about and walked toward the door. "Hain't goin' off mad, be you?"

"I don't know what to make of you, Dan," replied David. "A little while ago you gave me to understand that the reason why you wanted to bring the dog back to Don, was because you wanted to make everything square between you and him; and now you say you want to do it because Don has offered a reward for him."

"An' I told you the gospel truth both times," exclaimed Dan. "That thar animile is wuth every cent of fifty dollars; an' if I bring him back, it'll be that much in Don's pocket an' ten dollars in mine. I kin afford to work fur that, can't I?"

"Very well," said David. "If you will produce the dog, safe and sound, I'll take him to his master for you, and bring back the reward if he gives it to me."

This interview had a perceptible effect upon both the boys. It took away all Dan's industry, and all David's peace of mind. The former had gained his point. He had made his brother promise to take Dandy to his owner and bring back the reward, and that was happiness for one day. He didn't chop any more wood or take any more interest in the supper. He seated himself on the bench again and resumed the agreeable occupation in which he had spent the most of the afternoon - that of building air-castles.

David walked up and down the floor, with his hands in his pockets, thinking busily. He told himself over and over again that if it were not for his mother, he would not care if he should never see his home again. He was cheerful and happy when he was away from it, but it almost always happened that as soon as he crossed the threshold something transpired to make him miserable and gloomy. His conversation with Dan had confirmed a suspicion that had been lurking in his mind ever since the pointer disappeared. He had all the while held to the belief that Dan knew where the dog was, and Dan might as well have confessed it, for his face and his actions constantly betrayed him. David believed, too, that his father had not left the country, as a good many people in the settlement seemed to think, but that he was hiding in the woods somewhere in the immediate neighborhood. Of this he had received proof that was almost positive. He knew, if Don and Bert did not, that it was something besides a bear they had driven off Bruin's Island, on the day they went up the bayou with the hounds. He had seen footprints in the mud that were made by a barefooted man; and more than that, having been the first to come out of the cane when the dogs led the way toward the head of the island, he had caught a glimpse of something, as it was disappearing in the bushes on the main shore, which looked wonderfully like the tattered hickory shirt his father had worn the last time he saw him. This discovery, taken in connection with Dan's behavior, led David to believe that his father and brother were often in communication with each other; and when the pointer disappeared, he promptly settled it in his own mind that Godfrey and Dan were to blame for it. He was as certain now that Dan had had a finger in the business as he would have been if he had seen him going off with the dog; and he resolved that as soon as the next day dawned, he would take pains to find out whether or not he was correct in supposing that his father was Dan's accomplice.

"Father hid on Bruin's Island while the Yankees were raiding through here," thought David. "When we drove him off, thinking he was a bear, of course he had to hunt a new hiding-place, and it is possible that he is now camping close about there on the main shore. If I can find his camp, I'll take a good look at it. If I don't see the pointer there, well and good; I shall be very glad of it. But if he is there, I must get hold of him somehow. Don has been swindled out of enough money by the black sheep of our family, and he shan't lose any more by them if I can help it."

As this thought passed through David's mind, an expression of determination settled on his face, which did not fail to attract the notice of Dan, who just then happened to look into the cabin to see what his brother was doing.

"What you lookin' that ar way fur?" demanded Dan. "Ain't puttin' up a job on me, be you?"

David replied that he was not.

"You'll take the pinter to Don an' fetch me back the ten dollars, honor bright?" continued Dan.

"That is what I promised to do, isn't it?" asked David in reply. "But if I can help it you will never have the dog in your possession again," he added, mentally. "I didn't promise that I wouldn't head you off if I could."

"An' you won't answer no questions? Don said in that notice that he wouldn't ax none."

"Then of course I shall not answer any. You needn't be afraid. I shan't mention your name."

"Kase if you're thinkin' of puttin' up a job on me, Davy," said Dan, shaking his finger at his brother, "you won't never see that pinter ag'in so long as you live. Keep still now. Here comes the ole woman."

Dan settled back on the bench again, and David took his hands out of his pockets long enough to throw a fresh log of wood on the fire - not because it was needed, but for the reason that he wanted to hide his face from his mother for a minute or two until he could call to it a more cheerful expression than the one it was then wearing. He had never said a word to his mother about his suspicions regarding his father and Dan, for he wanted to talk to her about nothing but pleasant and agreeable things. She had enough to trouble her already.

David had everybody in the cabin up at an earlier hour than usual the next morning, and after eating a very hasty breakfast, he took his gun under his arm, bade his mother good-by and disappeared own the road that led to General Gordon's. Dan sat on the bench and watched him as long as he remained in sight.

"It's a heap easier to have a feller to 'arn your money fur you nor it is to 'arn it yourself," thought Dan. "Here's Dave a toilin' an' a slavin' fur them hundred an' fifty dollars, an' when he gets 'em, they'll go plump into pap's pocket an' mine, an' he'll never see no good of 'em at all. I'll have ten dollars in my pocket this very night. It's 'most too frosty to go slashin' round through the bushes now, so I'll wait till the sun gets a little higher, then I'll go arter that pinter."

David kept on down the road, until he was out of sight of the cabin, and then he climbed the fence and plunged into a dense thicket of briers, through which he made his way with great difficulty, following nearly the same path that Clarence Gordon followed on the morning he went through there to release his cousin Don from the potato-cellar. Reaching the woods at last, he took a straight course for Bruin's Island, and half an hour's rapid walking brought him within sight of it.

David's first care was to satisfy himself that it was a man and not a bear that Don's hounds had driven off the island; and in order to set all his doubts on this point at rest, he looked for the footprints which the man or animal must have made when he left the water and climbed the bank. David found the tracks after a few minutes' search, and a single glance at them confirmed his suspicions. They were made by a barefooted man, and that man must have been Godfrey Evans, for there was no one else in the settlement, that he knew of, who was so very anxious to escape observation that he was willing to swim a bayou on a cold day.

"I was right," said David to himself, feeling grieved and mortified when he remembered that his father had been hunted like a wild animal. "He is somewhere about here, and if I find him, I shall find the pointer with him. There he is now!"

The sharp crack of a rifle rang through the woods at that moment, and David scrambled up the bank and hurried away in the direction from which it sounded. He knew it was his father's gun (those who are experienced in such matters will tell you that there is as much difference in the reports of rifles as there is in the sound of the human voice), even before he received the proof that came a moment later. Scarcely had the report died away when he heard an impatient yelp just in front of him, and that he also recognised. It was uttered by Dandy. Godfrey was probably out hunting for his breakfast, and the pointer, excited by the report of the gun, was complaining because he was tied up in the camp and left behind. This was the way David explained the situation to himself, and the sequel proved that he was right.

After running through the bushes for a short distance, David came within sight of a little cloud of smoke, which ascended from a hollow just in advance of him. A few steps more brought him within sight of the camp, and the first object his eyes rested upon was Don Gordon's pointer, which was tied to a sapling near a little bark lean-to, something like the one Godfrey occupied while he was living on the island. The animal, hearing his approach, advanced to meet him as far as the length of his rope would allow, and stood wagging his tail with every demonstration of joy.

"I've saved Don ten dollars," thought David, as he pulled out his knife and cut the rope, "and I have kept Dan and father from playing a most contemptible trick upon one who would be a good friend to them, if they would only let him."

David had taken no pains to approach his father's camp without being discovered. He knew he was in the right, and he intended to be open and above board in everything he did. He expected to meet his father face to face, and he was ready to use every argument he could think of to induce him to surrender the pointer, that is, if the animal should be found in his possession. If arguments and entreaties failed, he was prepared to use other means, although he knew that by so doing he would bring certain punishment upon himself. Very fortunately, however, he chanced to reach the camp during his father's absence, and all he had to do was to liberate the pointer and go home with him.

"I'm glad it happened just as it did," thought David, drawing a long breath of relief; "I don't want to get into trouble with father, for I have seen him angry too many times. If he should catch me here now I believe he'd half kill me."

"Halloo, Dannie! What brung you up here so 'arly, an' whar be you goin' with the dog?"

David's heart seemed to stop beating, and his old single-barrel grew so heavy that he could scarcely sustain its weight. His first impulse was to take to his heels, but the unexpected sound of the familiar voice seemed to have deprived him of all power of motion. He did manage, however, to turn his head and look in the direction from which the voice sounded, and saw his father standing a little way off, with his rifle on his shoulder and a squirrel in his hand.

"Dave!" exclaimed the latter, so surprised that he could scarcely speak.

"Yes, it's Dave," replied the boy, who saw that the battle for which he had prepared himself was likely to come off after all.

"What business you got up here, an' how come you by that pinter pup?" demanded Godfrey.

"My business up here was to get the dog. I found him in your camp, and I cut him loose because I have a better right to him than you have."

"Wal, we'll see 'bout that thar," returned Godfrey, throwing down his squirrel and leaning his rifle against the nearest tree. David's face grew pale, for he knew what was coming now. His father's next move would be to reach for a hickory.

"Who told you I was up here?" demanded Godfrey, and David's uneasiness increased when he saw that his father was running his eyes over the bushes nearest him. He was picking out a good stout switch.

"No one told me," answered David.

"Then how did you know whar I was?"

"I was up here with Don and Bert on the day you swam the bayou, and I saw you just after you had climbed the bank and were dodging into the bushes."

"Don't you think you was a very grateful an' dutiful' son to hunt your poor ole pap outen a good hidin'-place an' make him take to the water like a hounded deer, in this cold weather too, an' my rheumatiz so bad?" asked Godfrey, angrily. "Who told you the pinter was here?"

"Nobody. I just guessed at it."

"Wal, what be you goin' to do with him, now you got him?"

"I'm going to take him back to his master and save him ten dollars."

"Ten dollars!" repeated Godfrey. "Is that what he's goin' to give to get him back? Now, Dave," and here Godfrey pulled out the hunting-knife which he always carried in a sheath attached to his bullet-pouch, and cut down the switch he had selected, "you jest take that thar pinter dog back whar you got him an' tie him up thar; you hear me?"

"I do, but I'll hold fast to the dog. You and Dan have swindled Don out of enough money already; and now I'll tell you what's a fact -"

David did not finish the sentence. He saw his father dash his hat upon the ground, and knowing what was coming, he faced about and took to his heels.

CHAPTER XIV

SOME DISCOVERIES

David would have been glad to reason with his father, but he had not been allowed the opportunity, and now it was too late to find one. His first thought was of the pointer. Giving the animal a hasty kick, to start him on his way home, David sought to save himself by flight, although he had little hope of success. Everybody said he was a swift runner for a boy of his age, and he did his best now, but fast as he went, Godfrey gained at every step. David heard his heavy footfalls growing louder and more distinct, and once or twice he lost all heart, and was on the point of stopping and surrendering at discretion. But he knew that the beating he would receive would be a most severe one, and he was sure he did not deserve it, and that his father had no business to give it to him. This thought lent him wings, and a few more jumps brought him to the bayou.

"I've got you now!" cried Godfrey, and David heard the switch whistle through the air, as his pursuer made an effort to reach him with it.

Godfrey thought the bayou would offer an effectual check to David's flight, but the boy himself looked upon it as his only means of escape. He ran straight to the bank, which at this point arose almost perpendicularly from the water to the height of at least twenty feet, and just as Godfrey was stretching forth his hand to seize him by the collar, he

Harry Castlemon

disappeared. His pursuer tried to stop himself, but so rapid was his flight that he made one or two involuntary steps, and it was only by catching hold of a friendly bush that he saved himself from following David over the bluff.

"Dog-gone my buttons!" thought Godfrey, gazing in astonishment at the bubbles on the surface of the water, which marked the spot where David had gone down. "Who'd a thought he would a jumped into the Bayou sooner nor take a leetle trouncin'? He's gettin' to be a powerful bad boy, Dave is, an' I had oughter be to hum every day to keep him straight. Come back here!" he shouted, as the fugitive's head suddenly bobbed up out of the water. "If you'll ketch the pinter fur me an' promise to say nothin' to nobody, I'll let you off this time."

David could not say a word in reply. He felt as if every drop of blood in his body had been turned into ice. He wiped the water from his eyes, glanced over his shoulder, to make sure that his father had not followed him into the bayou, and struck out for the opposite bank. Godfrey coaxed, promised and threatened to no purpose. David would not come back, and neither would he make any answer. He held as straight across the bayou as the current would permit, and when he reached the shore, he climbed out and disappeared in the bushes.

"He's gone," thought Godfrey, throwing away his switch and slowly retracing his steps toward the camp, "an' here's more trouble for me. The pinter's gone too, an' that takes money outen my pocket an' puts it into the pockets of them pizen Gordons. Dave'll tell everything he knows as soon as he gets hum, an' that'll bring the constable up here arter me. I must go furder back in the cane, but I won't go outen the settlement, an' nobody shan't drive me out nuther, till I get my hands onto them hundred an' fifty dollars. Then nobody won't ever hear of me ag'in - Dan nor none of 'em. It's jest a trifle comfortin' to know that that thar mean Dave can't do no more shootin'; he lost his gun."

Yes, David's faithful friend and companion was gone. It slipped from his grasp as he struck the water, and was now lying at the bottom of the bayou. He felt the loss as keenly as Don Gordon would have felt the loss of his fine breech-loader.

David thought he had never before been so nearly frozen as he was when he struck the opposite bank of the bayou; but a few minutes' vigorous exercise put his blood in circulation again, and then he began to feel more comfortable. He followed the bayou until he reached the lake, and then he plunged into the water again, and swam across to the other shore. It was cold work, but he had no boat, and so there was nothing else he could do. He was a very forlorn-looking object indeed, when he reached the cabin. Dan, who was still sunning himself on the bench, must have thought so, for when his brother first appeared in sight, he jumped up and stared at him as if he could not quite make up his mind whether the approaching object was David Evans, or one of the dreaded haunts that lived in the General's lane. He could not wholly satisfy himself on this point until he had made some inquiries. "Is that you your own self, Davy?" he asked, holding himself ready to take to his heels in case a satisfactory answer was not promptly returned.

David replied that it was.

"What's the matter of you, an' whar you been?" continued Dan. "Whar's your gun?"

"I have swam the bayou twice, and I have been taking a walk in the woods. My gun is in the water near the foot of Bruin's Island."

Dan opened his eyes and was about to propound a multitude of questions, when something that came around the corner of the cabin just then checked him. It was Don Gordon's pointer. He had found his way to the cabin and taken quiet possession of his bed in the kennel, and Dan was none the wiser for it until that moment. Hearing the sound of David's voice, the dog came out to meet him, and the two appeared to be over-joyed to see each other again. Dan opened his eyes wider than ever, and backed toward his seat on the bench without saying a word.

"I found him right where you left him, Dan," said David, who thought it high time his brother should know that some of his mean acts were being brought to light. "I've got him again, you see, and you'll never have another chance to steal him."

"What have you got, an' whar did I leave him?" Dan managed to ask at last.

"O, I wouldn't try to play off innocent, if I were you. I know all about it; and I want to tell you now that you had better turn over a new leaf and be quick about it, too. Mother says that if folks don't grow better every day, they grow worse, and I can see that it is true in your case and father's. You are both going down hill, and the first thing you know you'll do something that will get you in the calaboose. Three months ago neither one of you would have been guilty of stealing."

"Whoop!" yelled Dan, jumping up and knocking his heels together.

"I don't want to go back on either one of you," continued David, "and neither do I want to tell mother how bad you are; but I'll do it sooner than let you swindle Don Gordon or anybody else. Why don't you go to work?"

"Kase I've got jest as much right to set around an' do nothin' as other folks has," answered Dan, who had had time to recover himself in some measure. "That's jest why!"

"Mother and I don't sit around and do nothing."

"No, but them Gordons does."

"No, they don't. They all work, Don and Bert as well as the rest."

"If I hadn't seed them ridin' round so much on them circus hosses an' sailin' in them painted boats of their'n, mebbe I'd be willin' to b'lieve that," said Dan. "They don't work, nuther. They don't do nothin', but have good times. They've got good clothes an' nice things, an' I've got jest as much right to 'em as they have."

"Those ideas will get you into trouble some day," replied David, earnestly. "If you want nice things go to work and earn them; that's the way to get them."

While this conversation was going on, David was pulling off his wet clothes and putting on his best suit, the one he wore on Sundays. It was not just such a suit as the most of us would like to go to church in, but it was whole and neat, and David looked like another boy in it. He kept the pointer in the house with him all the while, for fear that his brother might attempt to steal him again; but Dan was too much astonished at the turn affairs were taking, and too badly frightened, to make any more efforts to win the ten dollars reward. He sat on the bench, with his eyes fastened thoughtfully on the ground, and saw David come out with the pointer and lead him down the road toward General Gordon's, without saying a word.

When David reached the barn he walked straight through it to the shop, and there he found Don and Bert, busy at work building more traps. They were surprised to see him dressed in his best, and still more surprised, and delighted too, when the pointer bounded in and fawned upon them.

"Father said that the offer of a reward would bring him if anything would," exclaimed Don, as he wound his arms around the animal's neck and hugged him as he might have hugged a brother he had not seen for a long time.

"Yes, the reward did it," replied David, and that was true. If

Dan had not seen the notice in the post-office, he never would have had that conversation with David, and consequently the latter would not have known where to go to find the pointer.

"We all thought he was stolen," continued Don. "I am glad you are the one to bring him back, for I would rather give you the ten dollars than give it to anybody else."

"I don't want the money," said David, "and I won't take it."

"You can't help yourself. Where did you find him?"

"Didn't you promise that you wouldn't ask any questions?" asked David, with a smile.

"Well - yes, I did," answered Don, somewhat astonished. "But I made that promise just to let the thief see that he would run no risk in returning the dog. I can question you, can't I?"

"I'd rather you wouldn't."

Don uttered a long-drawn whistle and looked at Bert to see what he thought about it; but the blank expression on the latter's face showed that he was altogether in the dark.

"Well, let it go," said Don, picking up his hammer again. "I've got the dog back and with that I'll be satisfied. You'll take him home with you tonight, of course?"

"No, I think not. I am afraid to take him there."

"Then leave him here," said Don, who now began to think that he knew pretty nearly what had been going on. "He'll be safe with us, and you can find him when you want him. He isn't broken yet."

"I know it, but I can't do any more for him. I shall have to give you back your ten dollars."

"I'll not take it. A bargain is a bargain. I want my dog broken, and you need the money to send off your quails with."

"I know it," said David again; "but I can't shoot any more birds over him. I have no gun."

"Where is it?"

"At the bottom of the bayou."

The brothers grew more and more astonished the longer they talked with David, and Don told himself that there had been some queer doings in the settlement that morning. His interest and curiosity were thoroughly aroused, but he did not ask any more questions, for he knew that David could not explain matters without exposing one or more members of his own family. He turned the conversation into a new channel by saying suddenly:

"Bert and I made the rounds of the traps this morning, and took out a hundred and fifty birds. What do you say to that?"

Under almost any other circumstances David would have had a good deal to say about it; but just now he seemed to have lost all interest in his business. It would have been hard for any boy to wear a merry smile and keep up a light heart after such a scene as David had passed through that morning. He could not banish it from his memory. His father was hiding in the woods, because he was afraid to show his face among his neighbors again; he was a receiver of stolen property and his brother Dan was a thief, and the remembrance of these facts was enough to depress the most buoyant spirits. David wanted to do something to bring his father and brother to their senses, and induce them to become decent, respected members of the community, but he did not know how to set about it, and there was no one of whom he could ask advice. He never talked to his mother about the family difficulties now. She had more than her share of trouble, and David always tried to talk about cheerful things when he was in her presence.

Harry Castlemon

"Doesn't it cheer you up any to know that your business is prospering?" exclaimed Bert. "Then we will tell you something else. How would you like to be mail carrier? How would you like to put thirty dollars in your pocket every month?"

"That is more money than I shall be able to earn for long years to come," replied David.

"Perhaps not. Father told us this morning that the old mail carrier is going to give up his route, his contract having expired, and he thinks he can get you appointed in his place. He's been to see Colonel Packard, and Silas Jones, and all the rest of the prominent men in the settlement, and they have promised to give you all their influence and to go on your bond."

"What does that mean?" asked David, who now began to show some interest in the matter.

"Why, there are certain legal forms to go through with, which father explained, but which I don't pretend to understand," said Bert. "You must promise to attend to your business -"

"O, I'll do that," exclaimed David.

"Of course you will," said Don, "but that will not satisfy the authorities in Washington. They don't know you, and even if they did it would make no difference. The law must be complied with, and you must give bonds for the faithful performance of your duty. But that needn't trouble you; father will attend to it. He says your chances are good, for you are the only one on the track so far."

This was the first time David knew that there was anybody on the track. He was greatly astonished and delighted, and his attempts to express his gratitude for the General's kindness and thoughtfulness were awkward enough. Thirty dollars was a large sum of money in his eyes. His earnings would amount to three hundred and sixty dollars a year, and couldn't he and his mother live nicely on that and save something for a rainy day besides? If he could get the contract, and his father and Dan would only abandon their lazy, worthless mode of life and go to work, how happy they would all be!

"What's the matter?" asked Don, for David's face became clouded again when he thought of his father and Dan.

"There's a good deal the matter," replied David, "but it is nothing I can help."

"You don't act like yourself at all to-day," continued Don. "Suppose you go home and take a rest. Don't brood over your troubles, whatever they are. Let them go, if you can't help them. Think about pleasant things, and to-morrow you will come up here, feeling like a new boy. Bert and I will set the traps we have made this morning, and then we'll go up and take a look at our bear trap."

David thought it would be a good plan to follow this advice, so he closed the door of the shop to keep the pointer from following him, and started for home.

"Well," said Bert, as he picked up his knife and resumed work upon the figure four he was making, "Dave has seen his father!"

"And had trouble with him, too," added Don.

"It was about the pointer," said Bert.

"My idea exactly. Godfrey is hiding somewhere in the cane; Dan wanted to make a little more money without work, so he stole the pointer and gave him to his father to keep until I offered a reward for him. David found it out, and to save me from being swindled, he recovered the pointer and got himself into difficulty by it."

The boys, who were merely guessing at all this, would have

been surprised to know that their surmises were all correct. David and his troubles, and his manful efforts to better his condition in spite of his adverse circumstances, afforded them topics of conversation while they were at work; and when the figure four, on which Bert was employed, was completed, the mule was harnessed to the wagon, and the boys drove off to set the half a dozen new traps they had built that morning. It was twelve o'clock when they returned, and they found lunch waiting for them. When they had done ample justice to it, they began making hasty preparations for their visit to the island, and a quarter of an hour more saw them well on their way up the bayou.

They found to their great delight that the ducks were beginning to come in now, and Don was kept busy rowing from one side of the bayou to the other to pick up the dead and wounded birds that Bert brought out of the numerous flocks which took wing as they approached. After a dozen fine fat mallards had been brought to bag, Bert declared that it was a sin to shoot any more, and took his place at the oars, while Don sat in the stern and steered.

"These ducks tell us that it is time to go to our shooting-box," said the latter. "We always wait until they begin to come in before we make up our party, you know."

"We ought to go over there and fix up a bit first," said Bert. "If we don't find anything in our trap, let's go over there and see how things look. We have had some splendid times in that little shooting-box, haven't we?"

They certainly had, and they found much pleasure in living them over again in imagination. While they were talking about the many happy hours they had spent there, they reached Bruin's Island, and Don brought the canoe around and ran the bow upon the beach. The hounds jumped out, and running about with their noses close to the ground, began to show the same signs of excitement that they had exhibited on the day of their first visit to the island. The boys knew more now than they did then, and consequently were not in such haste to declare that it was a bear the dogs scented. It might be Godfrey Evans; and that he or somebody else had been there since they left was very evident. Their trap had been sprung by the aid of a long pole, which was still fast under the heavy roof; the lever and rope had been carried away; and the bag of corn which Don had hung upon the sapling had also disappeared. Don was provoked, and laid up in his mind a few sharp words, to be addressed to Godfrey on the subject, should they ever happen to meet again; but he had very little to say. The boys had been thoughtful enough to bring an axe, a piece of rope and another small bag of corn with them, and, although they had no assurance that their labor would not be wasted, they set the trap again and started for home.

"If Godfrey did that," said Don, "he must have swam the bayou, unless he has a boat hidden away in the bushes somewhere, which is not likely. If it was summer now, he would probably spring that trap every day, just to keep us from catching that bear; but the weather is getting frosty, and he'll not relish many more cold baths. I don't think he will trouble us that way any more."

When they reached the mouth of the bayou, Bert, who was steering, directed the canoe across the lake, toward the point on which the shooting-box was located. During a pause in the conversation, he looked toward the place where it ought to be, but could see nothing of it. "What's the matter?" asked his brother, who saw that there was something wrong.

"That's Long Point, isn't it?" asked Bert, in reply. "It certainly is, but where's the house?"

"You haven't been there in almost six months, and perhaps you have forgotten where it is," said Don, with a laugh.

"No, I haven't. It stood close beside a big shell-bark, didn't it? Well, there's the tree; now show me the shooting-box?"

Harry Castlemon

Don faced about on his seat, expecting to point the building out to his brother at once, and was a good deal surprised when he found that he could not see it himself. There was the tree, sure enough, but the spot which the shooting-box ought to have occupied, was vacant. After running his eyes all along the shore, to satisfy himself that he had made no mistake as to the locality, Don picked up the oars again, and with a few more strokes brought the canoe to the bank. All there was left of the shooting-box they could have carried away in their arms. Even the stove had not escaped destruction. The chimney had fallen upon it and it was completely ruined.

"Godfrey means to put a stop to all our fun if he can, doesn't he?" said Bert, who thought that a man who would steal a canoe and spring a trap, would be guilty of any meanness.

"Let's go home," was Don's reply. "We'll have another shooting-box here some day, Bert, and it will beat the old one all to pieces."

The boys thought they had had hard luck that day, and so did their father, when he had heard their story; but they came very near having worse luck that night, and they never knew anything about it until several days afterward. The General found it out the next morning. He went to the fields at an early hour, as he always did, to set his negroes at work, and was met by the hostler, who had an exciting piece of news to communicate. "Misser Gordon," said he, "Misser Don's hound dogs done treed two fellers down dar in de quarter. Dey's been dar all de blessed night top o' dat ar house; yes, sar, dat's what dey says, sar!"

The General replied that if the two fellows had come there for the purpose of stealing, he was glad of it, and said he would go and take a look at them. When he saw them, perhaps he would know where the contents of his smoke-house had been going lately. He rode down to the quarters as soon as his horse was brought out, and when he came within sight of the cabin in which the boys kept their captured quails, he saw two persons sitting astride of the ridge-pole and Don's hounds gathered about the building, keeping guard over them. The General could scarcely believe his eyes, although when he came to recall several little things which Don and Bert had told him, he was not so very much surprised after all. The persons whom the hounds had forced to take refuge on the roof of the cabin were boys; and as soon as the General was near enough to them to distinguish their features, he saw that they were Lester Brigham and Bob Owens.

CHAPTER XV

BOB'S ASPIRATIONS

"I think it my duty to inform you that the parties to whom you have given your order for fifty dozen live quails will certainly disappoint you. They did not seek the contract for themselves, but for another person, who knows nothing whatever about trapping, and who is much too indolent to put forth the necessary exertion if he did. You will get no birds from him. If, after waiting a reasonable time - I should think two weeks would be long enough - you become satisfied of this fact, I shall be happy to receive your order, and will guarantee you satisfaction."

This was a rough copy of the letter Lester drew up to send to the advertiser in the "*Rod and Gun*," on the evening of the day on which he held that interview with Don and Bert, when the former refused to join his sportsman's club. He read it to Bob in his best style and was astonished when his friend declared that it wouldn't do at all. "You seem to forget that I am working for a new shot-gun," said Bob. "The language isn't half strong enough."

"You can't improve it anywhere," replied Lester, who was rather proud of the production. "Do you want me to abuse Don and the rest? That would be poor policy, for the man would say right away that we were jealous of them and trying to injure them. I have told him that he will get no birds from David, and if he does, it will be our fault."

Bob could not see the force of this reasoning. There was so much at stake that it was necessary they should do everything in their power to secure the contract, and he was sure it would help matters if a few hard words were added respecting Don and David. So they were put in, and the letter was copied and dropped into the post-office.

After that Lester took up his abode with Bob Owens. According to an agreement made between them, Bob went through the ceremony of sending a note to Lester by a negro boy, inviting him to come over and spend a week with him, bringing his horse and gun, and they would have a fine time shooting turkeys and driving the ridges for deer. This arrangement enabled the two conspirators to be together day and night. They intended to pass the most of their time in riding about through the woods, and if a deer or turkey happened to come in their way and they should be fortunate enough to shoot it, so much the better; but if the game kept out of their sight they would not spend any precious moments in looking for it. Their object was to devote themselves exclusively to destroying all David's chances for earning the hundred and fifty dollars. They would watch him closely, and when they found out where his traps were set, they would visit them daily, and steal every quail they found in them.

During the first few days the boys spent together they found out two things: one was that there was a pile of traps in the yard behind Godfrey Evans's cabin, and that they were never touched except when the family happened to be in want of kindling wood. The other was, that David left home bright and early every morning and went straight to General Gordon's. What he did after he got there they could not find out. They would always wait an hour or two to see if he came out again, and then they would grow tired of doing nothing, and spend the rest of the day searching the woods and brier-patches in the neighborhood of the cabin, in the hope of finding some of David's traps. But they never found a single one, for the reason that they were all set on the General's plantation, and the boys never thought of looking there for them.

"It's my opinion," said Lester, one day, when the two were seated at a camp-fire in the woods, broiling a brace of squirrels which Bob had shot, "that David has given it up as a bad job and left the way clear for us."

"Hurrah!" shouted Bob.

"Well - yes; but I'd hurrah louder if he had only set a dozen or two traps and given us a chance to rob them. If he'd done that, we might have had a hundred birds on hand now. The best thing we can do is to set our own traps and catch the quails as fast as we can. We'll keep an eye on David all the same, however."

This programme was duly carried out - that is, they spent the rest of the day in setting their traps, but they did not devote any more time to watching David's movements. Two incidents happened within a few hours that suggested new ideas to them, and made them sure that at last they had the game in their own hands. They had built a good many traps, and having no mule and wagon at their command, as Don Gordon had, it took them all the rest of the day to set them, so that it was dark by the time they reached home. They found the family at supper and listening with great interest and attention to something Mr. Owens was saying.

Mr. Owens was like Godfrey Evans in two respects. His ideas ran just as far ahead of his income as Godfrey's did, and he hated those who were better off in the world than himself. Especially did he dislike General Gordon. The latter was looked up to by all the best people as the leading man in the community, and that was something Mr. Owens could not endure. He wanted that honor himself; and because he could not have it, he made it a point to oppose and injure the General in every possible way.

"What do you think Gordon is trying to do now?" Mr. Owens

asked, just as the boys came in and took their seats at the table. "Gardner's mail contract has run out, and as he doesn't intend to put in another bid, that meddlesome Silas Jones asked the General who would be a good man to take his place; and Gordon hadn't any more sense than to recommend Dave Evans."

"Well, of all the things I ever heard of!" exclaimed Bob.

"That's what I thought," continued Mr. Owens. "I heard them talking about it at the post-office. Gordon was as busy as a candidate on election day. He was going around speaking to all the men about it, and asking them if they would lend their influence to secure the contract for David, and, although I put myself in his way two or three times, he never said a word to *me*. I suppose he thought my influence didn't amount to anything one way or the other, but perhaps he'll see his mistake some day."

"What's the pay, father?" asked Bob.

"Thirty dollars a month was Gardner's bid, and he rode the route only twice each week. But he had to go rain or shine. How would you like it, Bob?"

"The best in the world!" exclaimed the boy, eagerly. "Three hundred and sixty dollars a year! Couldn't I sport just as fine a hunting and fishing rig as anybody? Can't you get it for me, father?"

"I was thinking about it on the way home, and I made up my mind that I could try. Gordon thinks he holds the whole state of Mississippi under his thumb, but he hasn't got me there."

"Nor my father, either," said Lester. "He'll help you, Mr. Owens."

"I was counting on him. When I send in the application, I'll have to send a bond for a few hundred dollars with it."

"Father will go on it, if I ask him, and I will, for I'll do anything to help Bob and beat that beggar, Dave Evans."

The conversation continued for an hour or more in this strain, and when the boys had heard David and all his friends soundly abused, and Bob had provided for the spending of every cent of the money he would earn during the first year he rode the route, if his father succeeded in obtaining the appointment for him, he and Lester went out to attend to their horses and talk the matter over by themselves. Bob was in ecstacies; and while he was counting off on his fingers the various articles he intended to purchase with his wages, Lester suddenly laid his hand on his arm.

"What's that?" said he, in a suppressed whisper.

Bob looked in the direction indicated by his companion, and saw a dark figure creeping stealthily along the fence. His actions plainly showed that he had no business there, and, as if moved by a common impulse, the two boys dropped to the ground and waited to see what he was going to do.

"It's some thieving nigger," whispered Bob. "If he lays a hand on anything we'll jump up and catch him."

"Hadn't I better go into the house and call your father?" asked Lester.

"O, no; you and I can manage him. Do you see those fence pickets over there? Well, we'll sneak up and get one apiece, and then if he attempts any resistance, we shall be ready for him."

The pickets, of which Bob spoke, were piled about twenty yards nearer to the barn than the boys then were, and they succeeded in creeping up to them and arming themselves without attracting the notice of the prowler. The latter followed the fence until he reached a point opposite the spot where the barn, corn-cribs and other out-buildings were located, and there he stopped to survey the ground before him.

Having made sure that there was no one in sight, he moved quickly toward the smokehouse and tried the door.

"I don't think you'll make much there, my friend," whispered Bob. "That door is locked."

The prowler found it so, and after a few ineffectual attempts to force it open by pushing with his shoulder against it, he faced about and disappeared in the barn. While the boys were trying to make up their minds whether or not they ought to run up and corner him there, he came out again, and he did not come empty-handed either. He carried a bag of meal on his shoulder - the one Mr. Owens had put in the barn that morning for the use of his horses - and in his hand something that looked like a stick of stove-wood; but it was in reality a strong iron strap, which he had found in the barn and which he intended to use to force an entrance into the smokehouse. He deposited his bag of meal upon the ground, set to work upon the hasp with his lever and in a few minutes more the door swung open.

"Now is our time," whispered Bob, as the robber disappeared in the smoke-house. "Stand by me and we'll have a prisoner when we go back to the house."

Lester would have been very glad indeed to have had some excuse for remaining in his place of concealment, and allowing his companion to go on and capture the robber alone; but he could not think of any, and when Bob jumped up and ran toward the smoke-house, Lester followed him, taking care, however, to regulate his pace so that his friend could keep about ten or fifteen feet in advance of him. Bob, who was in earnest and not in the least alarmed, moved with noiseless footsteps, while Lester, preferring to let the robber escape rather than face him with no better weapon than a fence picket in his hand, made all the noise he conveniently could, hoping that the man would take the alarm and run out of the smoke-house before they could reach it. But the thief was so busily engaged that he did not hear their approach, and never dreamed of danger until the boys halted in front of the door and ordered him to come out and give himself up. We ought rather to say that Bob halted in front of the door and boldly stood his ground there, while Lester took care to shelter himself behind the building, and showed only the top of his cap to the robber.

"We've got you now, you rascal!" exclaimed Bob, bringing his club against the side of the smokehouse with a sounding whack. "Come out and surrender yourself, or we'll come in and take you out."

"Yes," chimed in Lester, in a trembling voice, at the same time hitting the building a very feeble blow with his fence picket. "Come out, and be quick about it. There are a dozen of us here, enough to make -"

Lester finished the sentence with a prolonged shriek of terror, for just then something that seemed to move with the speed and power of a lightning express train, dashed out of the intense darkness which concealed all objects in the interior of the smoke-house, and Lester received a glancing blow on the shoulder that floored him on the instant. While the latter was calling upon the robber to surrender, Bob heard a slight rustling in the smoke-house, and knowing very well what it meant, he jumped back out of the door-way, and raised his club in readiness to strike; but the thief was out and gone before he could think twice. The instant the robber landed on his feet outside the door, he turned toward the place where he had left his bag of meal and happened to come into collision with Lester, who went down with a jar that made him think every bone in his body was broken. It was a minute or two before he could collect his scattered wits and raise himself to his feet, and then he found that he was alone. Bob was scudding across the field in pursuit of the robber, who carried a side of bacon on one shoulder and the bag of meal on the other; but burdened as he was he ran quite fast enough to distance Bob, who presently came back to the smoke-house, panting and almost exhausted.

"Is he gone?" asked Lester, who was groping about on the ground in search of his club.

"I should say he was," Bob managed to reply. "He ran like a deer. He knocked you flatter than a pancake, didn't he?"

"He didn't hurt me as badly as I hurt him," said Lester. "Did you hear my club ring on his head?"

"No, but I heard you yell. You didn't strike him."

"What's the reason I didn't? I did, too, but it must have been a glancing blow, for if I had hit him fairly, I should have knocked him flatter than he knocked me. I yelled just to frighten him."

"I guess you succeeded, for I never saw a man run as he did. He got away, and he took the meal and bacon with him. They'll not do him any good, however, for he'll be in the calaboose by this time to-morrow, if there are men enough in the settlement to find him. I know him."

"You do? Who was he?"

"Godfrey Evans. He's been hiding in the cane ever since he and Clarence Gordon got into that scrape, and no one has ever troubled him. But somebody will trouble him now. I'll tell my father of it the first thing. I wonder how Dave will feel when he sees his father arrested and packed off to jail."

"I wouldn't do anything of the kind, if I were you," said Lester.

"You wouldn't?" cried Bob, greatly astonished. "Well, I won't let this chance to be revenged on Dave slip by unimproved, now I tell you."

"We can take revenge in a better way than that. We've got just as good a hold on him now as we want, and we'll make him promise that he will make no effort to catch those quails."

"O, I am no longer interested in that quail business," said Bob, loftily. "I'd rather have three hundred and sixty dollars than seventy-five."

"But you must remember that you haven't been appointed mail carrier yet, so you are by no means sure of your three hundred and sixty dollars. And even if you were, it would be worth your while to earn the seventy-five dollars, if you could, for that amount of money isn't to be found on every bush."

Lester went on to tell his friend of a bright idea that had just then occurred to him, and before he had fully explained how the events of the night could be made to benefit them, he had won Bob over to his way of thinking. The latter promised that he would say nothing to his father about the theft of which Godfrey had been guilty, until he and Lester had first told David of it and noted the effect it had upon him. If they could work upon his feelings sufficiently to induce him to give up the idea of trapping the quails, well and good. Godfrey might have the meal and bacon, and welcome. But if David was still obstinate and refused to listen to reason, they would punish him by putting the officers of the law on his father's track.

"It is a splendid plan and it will work, I know it will," exclaimed Bob, in great glee. "It will be some time before my appointment - those folks in Washington move very slowly - and while I am waiting for it, I may as well make seventy-five dollars. I can get my shot-gun with it, and spend my three hundred and sixty for the other things I need."

Bob slept but little that night for excitement, and dreaming about the glorious things that might be in store for him, kept him awake. He and Lester were up long before the sun, and as soon as they had eaten breakfast, they mounted their horses and rode off in the direction of Godfrey Evans's house. Early as it was when they arrived there, they found the cabin deserted by all save Dan, who sat on the bench by the door.

David was hastening through the woods toward his father's camp, intent on finding the pointer, and Mrs. Evans had gone to her daily labor.

"He's just went over to the General's house, Dave has," said Dan, in reply to a question from Lester; and he thought he told the truth, for we know that David went in that direction on purpose to mislead his brother. "Yes, he's went up thar, an' 'tain't no ways likely that he'll be to hum afore dark."

The visitors turned their horses about and rode away, and as soon as they were out of sight of the cabin, they struck into the woods to make one more effort to find David's traps, if he had set any. But, as usual, they met with no success, and Lester again gave it as his opinion, that David had no intention of trying to trap the quails. Bob thought so too; but in less than half an hour, they received positive proof that they were mistaken. They were riding around the rear of one of the General's fields, on their way home, when they happened to cast their eyes through the bushes that lined the fence, and saw something that surprised them greatly, and caused them to draw rein at once. There was a wagon in the field, and Don and Bert Gordon were passing back and forth between it and a little thicket of bushes and briers that stood a short distance away. They left the wagon with empty hands, and when they came back, they brought their arms full of something, which they stowed away in a box. While Lester and Bob were looking at them, a small, dark object suddenly arose from the box and came toward them, passing swiftly over their heads and disappearing in the woods.

"That's a quail!" exclaimed Bob. "It escaped from Don's hands."

"Yes, sir, and we have made a discovery," said Lester. "Dave Evans hasn't given up trapping the quails after all. He's catching them every day, and Don and Bert are helping him."

"It's just like them," replied Bob, in great disgust. "They're always poking their noses into other people's business. But I don't feel as badly over it as I did a short time ago."

"I know what you are counting on. You are as sure of that mail carrier's berth as you would be if you were to ride the route for the first time to-day; but if you should happen to slip up on it, you'd be glad to have the seventy-five dollars to fall back on."

"O, I am willing to work for it," replied Bob, quickly, "not only because I want it myself, but because I don't want Dave Evans to have it. What's to be done?"

"That trap must have been as full as it could hold," said Lester, thoughtfully. "They have made five or six trips between the wagon and that clump of bushes since we have been here. We know where one of the traps is set now, and that will guide us in finding the rest. When we do find them, we'll carry out our plan of robbing them every day. They must have trapped some birds before, and if we watch them when they go home we can find out where they keep them. What do you say to that?"

Bob replied that he was willing, and so the two dismounted, and having hitched their horses, set themselves to watch the wagon. They followed it at a respectful distance, as it made the rounds of the traps (they did not know that they also were followed by somebody, who kept a sharp eye on all their movements), and Bob grew angry every time he saw more quails added to those already in the coop.

"Those fellows are always lucky," he growled. "I'll warrant that if we visit those traps we set yesterday, we'll not find a single bird in them. Don and Bert are hauling them in by dozens."

"So much the better for us," returned his companion. "Every quail they catch makes it just so much easier for us to earn seventy-five dollars apiece."

Bob, feeling somewhat mollified by this view of the case, turned his attention to Don and his brother, who, having visited all their traps by this time, climbed into the wagon and drove toward home.

Harry Castlemon

CHAPTER XVI

DON'S HOUNDS TREE SOMETHING

Lester and his companion followed the wagon at a safe distance and saw it driven to the negro quarters, which were located about half a mile below the General's house. It stopped in front of one of the cabins, and Don and Bert began the work of transferring the quails from the coop to the building in which they were to remain until they were sent up the river. Bob and Lester counted the number of trips they made between the wagon and the door of the cabin, and made a rough estimate of the number of birds they had caught that morning.

"They've got at least a hundred," said Lester, when the wagon was driven toward the house, "and that is just one-sixth of the number they want. At that rate that beggar Dave will be rich in a week more."

"Not if we can help it!" exclaimed Bob, angrily. "That cabin will burn as well as the shooting-box did!"

"But we don't want to do too much of that sort of work," answered Lester. "We may get the settlement aroused, and that wouldn't suit us. I'd rather steal the birds, wouldn't you?"

Bob replied that he would, but hinted that if they attempted it they might have a bigger job on their hands than they had bargained for. In the first place, there were Don's hounds.

"But we braved them once - that was on the night we borrowed Don's boat to go up and burn his shooting-box - and we are not afraid to do it again," said Lester. "We didn't alarm them then."

Bob acknowledged the fact, but said he was afraid they might not be so lucky the next time. And even if they succeeded in breaking into the cabin without arousing the dogs, how were they to carry away a hundred live quails? The only thing they could do would be to put them in bags, and it was probable that half of them would die for want of air before they could get them home. They would be obliged to make two or three trips to the cabin in order to secure them all, and each time they would run the risk of being discovered by the hounds.

While the two friends were talking these matters over, they were walking slowly toward the place where they had left their horses. Having mounted, they started for home again, and the very first person they saw when they rode out of the woods into the road was David Evans, who had just been up to the shop to restore the pointer to his owner.

"There he is!" said Bob, in a low whisper. "He is dressed up in his best, too."

"Best!" sneered Lester. "Why, I wouldn't be seen at work in the fields in such clothes as those!"

"Nor in any other, I guess. They are the best he can afford," said Bob, who had some soft spots in his heart, if he was a bad boy, "and I don't believe in making fun of him."

"You believe in cheating him out of a nice little sum of money though, if you can," retorted Lester.

"No, I don't. I am working to keep him from cheating *me* out of it. If he will keep his place among the niggers, where fellows of his stamp belong, I'll be the last one to say or do anything against him; but when he tries to shove himself up among white folks, and swindle me out of a new shot-gun and get appointed mail carrier over my head, it's something I won't stand. Say, Dave," he added, drawing rein, as the subject of his remarks approached, "can you spare us just about two minutes for a little private conversation?"

"I reckon," replied David. "Have you joined that sportsman's club, and are you going to prosecute me for being a pot-hunter?"

"Lester has already told you what we are going to do about that, and you may rest assured that we shall *do* it," answered Bob, sharply. "What we say, we always stand to. What we want to talk to you about now is this: We know, as well as you do, that your father is hiding out here in the cane, and that he dare not show himself in the settlement for fear he will be arrested. You wouldn't like to see him sent to jail, would you?"

"I know what you mean," replied David. "My father may have been foolish, but he has done nothing that the law can touch him for."

When he said this he was thinking of Clarence Gordon and the barrel with the eighty thousand dollars in it. He did not know that Godfrey was guilty of highway robbery, and he forgot that he had also committed an assault upon Don, and that he had received and cared for stolen property, knowing it to be stolen.

"Hasn't he, though!" cried Bob. "He got into my father's smoke-house last night and stole some meal and bacon. He forced a lock to do it, too. The law can touch him for that, can't it?"

David leaned against the fence and looked at the two boys without speaking. He did not doubt Bob's story. He had been expecting to hear of such things for a long time. He had told himself more than once that when his father grew tired of living on squirrels, somebody's smoke-house and corn-crib would be sure to suffer. Godfrey was getting worse every day, and something told David that he would yet perform an act that would set every man in the settlement on his track.

"We can send him to prison," continued Bob. "You would not like that, of course, and you can prevent it if you feel like it. Lester and I are the only ones who know that he robbed my father last night, and we will keep it to ourselves on one condition."

"I know what it is," said David. "You want me to promise that I will trap no more quails. Perhaps you want the money yourselves."

"That's the very idea," said Lester.

"It isn't the money we care about," exclaimed Bob, quickly. "We've set out to put down this business of trapping birds and shipping them out of the country, and we're going to do it. You think that because Don and Bert are backing you up, you can do just as you please; but we'll show you that they don't run this settlement. You're getting above your business, Dave, and it is high time you were taught a lesson you will remember the longest day you live. What do you say? Will you trap any more quails?"

"Yes, I will," replied David, without an instant's hesitation.

"Don't forget that we can put the constable on your father's track to-morrow morning," said Bob, his voice trembling with rage.

"I wasn't thinking of my father. He has made his bed and he must lie in it. I was thinking of my mother. She must have something to eat and wear this winter, and how is she to get it, if I give up this chance of making a little money?"

"Just listen to you, now!" Bob almost shouted. "One would think to hear you talk that you are used to handling greenbacks by the bushel. You are a pretty looking ragamuffin to call a hundred and fifty dollars 'a little money,' are you not? It's more than your old shantee and all you've got in it are worth. Go on!" he yelled, shaking his riding whip at David, as the latter hurried down the road toward home. "I'll send you word when to come down to the landing and see your father go off to jail."

"I never saw such independence exhibited by a fellow in his circumstances," said Lester, as he and Bob rode away together. "One would think he was worth a million dollars."

"He thinks he will soon be worth a hundred and fifty, and that's what ails him," answered Bob, whose face was pale with fury. "But there's many a slip 'twixt the cup and the lip, as he will find before he is many days older. I'll tell my father to-night what Godfrey Evans did, and as soon as it grows dark we'll go down to that cabin and carry off all the birds we can catch. The rest we will liberate."

A part of this programme was duly carried out. As soon as they reached home Bob told his father what had happened the night before, and was a good deal surprised as well as disgusted, because Mr. Owens did not grow very angry, and declare that Godfrey should be punished to the full extent of the law.

"A bag of meal and a side of bacon are hardly worth making a fuss about," said Bob's father. "I will put a new lock on the smoke-house. But how does it come that you boys did not tell me of this at once?"

"Because we wanted to make something out of it," replied Bob. "If it hadn't been for Dave, Lester and I would have pocketed a nice little sum of spending money; but he's gone and got the job of trapping the quails, or rather that meddlesome Don Gordon got it for him, and, not satisfied with that, he has the cheek to run against me when I am trying to be appointed mail carrier."

"Well," said Mr. Owens.

"Well," repeated Bob, "I told him his father was a thief, and I could prove it, but I would say nothing about it if he would agree not to trap any more quails. If he had done that, I should have brought up this matter of carrying the mail, and made him promise to leave me a clear field there, too; but he wouldn't listen to anything."

"I am glad you told me this," said Mr. Owens, after thinking a moment, "and it is just as well that you did not say anything to David about the mail. No one knows that I am going to put in a bid for the contract, and I don't want it known; so be careful what you say. Gordon will never get that mail route for David, for the authorities will think twice before appointing the son of a thief to so responsible a situation."

"But are you going to do nothing to Godfrey?"

"I'll keep him in mind, and if it becomes necessary I'll put the constable after him, and tell him that the more fuss he makes in capturing him, the better it will suit me."

The first thing the two boys did after they had eaten their dinner, was to fit up one of the unoccupied negro cabins for the reception of the birds they intended to steal that night. There were a good many holes to be patched in the roof where the shingles had been blown off, and numerous others to be boarded up in the walls where the chinking had fallen out, and the afternoon was half gone before their work was done. They still had time to visit their traps, but all the birds they took out of them could have been counted on the fingers of one hand. Bob looked at them a moment, then thought of the big box full he had seen Don and Bert take home that morning, and grew very angry over his ill luck. He proposed to wring the necks of the captives and have them served up for breakfast the next morning, but Lester would not consent. Every one helped, he said, and these five birds, added to the forty or fifty they were to steal that night, would make a good start toward the fifty dozen they wanted.

After the boys had eaten supper, they secured four meal bags, which they hid away in a fence corner, so that they could find them again when they wanted them, and then adjourned to the wagon-shed to lay their plans for the night's campaign. Of course their expedition could not be undertaken until everybody about the General's plantation was abed and asleep. That would not be before ten or twelve o'clock - the negroes kept late hours since they gained their freedom, Bob said - and they dared not go to sleep for fear that they would not awake again before morning. They hardly knew what to do with themselves until bed time came. They spent an hour in talking over their plans, then went into the house and played checkers, and were glad indeed when the hour for retiring arrived. They made a show of going to bed, but they removed nothing but their boots, which they slammed down on the floor with more noise than usual. They heard the clock in the kitchen strike every hour, and when it struck twelve they began to bestir themselves.

Bob's room being located on the first floor, in one of the wings of the house, it was a matter of no difficulty for him and his companion to leave it without arousing any of the family. All they had to do was to open one of the windows, drop to the ground, pull on their boots and be off; and this they did in about the same time that it takes to tell it. They picked up their meal bags as they passed along the fence, and in half an hour more were inside General Gordon's fence, and moving cautiously along the lane that led toward the negro quarters. A few steps brought them into the midst of the cabins, which were as dark and silent as though they had been deserted. Some of them were deserted, while others were occupied by the field hands. The one in which the quails were confined stood on the outskirts of the quarters, and Bob, who had taken particular pains to mark the building, so that he would know it again, had no difficulty in finding it. It was the only cabin that was provided with a covered porch; and that same porch, or rather the posts which supported the roof, came very handy to the young prowlers a few minutes later. They walked around the building two or three times to make sure that there was no one near it, and then Bob cautiously mounted the steps and tried the door. The patter of little feet and the shrill notes of alarm that sounded from the inside told him that he had aroused the prisoners.

"Just listen to that," whispered Lester, greatly amazed. "The cabin must be full of them."

"We'll soon know how many there are," answered Bob. "I'd give something if I could see Don Gordon's face when he comes down here in the morning."

As Bob spoke, he opened one of the meal bags and drew from it the iron strap, which Godfrey Evans had used in prying open the door of the smoke-house two nights before. Lester struck a match on his coat sleeve, and when it blazed up, so that Bob could see how to work, he placed the strap between the hasp and the door, and exerted all his strength in the effort to draw out the staple with which it was confined. But that staple was put there to stay. It was made by the plantation blacksmith under Don's personal supervision, and as it was long enough to be clinched on the inside of the door, Bob made no progress whatever in his efforts to force an entrance.

"We can do nothing here," said he, after he had pulled and pushed until the inside of his hands seemed to be on fire. "We must try the window."

"But that is so high you can't reach it," said Lester.

"Not from the ground, I know. You will have to hold me up."

Descending from the porch with noiseless footsteps, the boys passed around to the rear of the cabin, and when Lester had stationed himself under the window, Bob quickly mounted to his shoulders. He examined the window as well as he could in the dark, and began to grow discouraged. It was boarded up with two-inch planks, and they were held in their places by the largest spikes Don could find at Mr. Jones's store. Bob pushed his lever under one of the planks, but when he laid out his strength upon it, Lester rocked about in so alarming a manner, that Bob lost his balance, and to save himself from falling, jumped to the ground.

"We might as well go home," said he, rubbing his elbow, which, owing to Lester's unsteadiness, he had scratched pretty severely on the rough planks. "If we only had a bundle of straw we'd start a bonfire."

"It's a pity to go home and leave all these birds here," replied Lester. "Let's get up on the roof and tear off some of the shingles. We can climb up by those posts that support the roof of the porch."

"O, it is easy enough to get up there, but what good will it do to tear off the shingles? We couldn't get the birds out unless one of us went down after them, and it wouldn't be me, I tell you!"

"We'll not try to get the birds at all. We'll leave the holes open so that they can escape. Wouldn't that be better than allowing them to stay here for Dave Evans to make money out of?"

"I should say it would," exclaimed Bob, who always grew angry whenever anything was said about David's chances of making money. "But we'll first make one more effort to get the birds ourselves. Hold me up again and don't wobble about as you did before."

In a few seconds more Bob was again perched upon his companion's shoulders, and this time he was sure that his efforts would be crowned with success. The planks were fastened to the window casing, which, on one side, was too badly decayed to hold the spikes. He started some of them with the first pull he made at his lever, and, encouraged by his progress, was about to prepare for a greater effort, when Lester uttered an exclamation of alarm and jumped from under him.

"Great Moses!" exclaimed Bob, who came to the ground with fearful violence. "Do you want to kill a fellow?"

"No," said Lester, whose voice trembled so that it was almost inaudible. "There's somebody coming!"

Before Bob could ask any more questions, a loud, shrill whistle, which sounded only a little distance away, rang through the quarters, followed almost immediately by the impatient yelp of a hound. The young prowlers were frightened almost out of their senses. Before they could make up their minds what ought to be done, a voice shouted:

"Here they be! Take 'em, fellers! Take 'em down!"

Another impatient yelp and the rush of feet on the hard road told the boys that Don Gordon's hounds were coming. This aroused them, and showed them the necessity of making an effort to escape. It was useless to run; the only place of safety was the roof of the cabin, and they made the most frantic efforts to reach it. They darted quickly around the corner of the building, sprang upon the porch and squirmed up the posts with the agility of monkeys. But with all their haste they did not have a second to spare. They had scarcely left the porch before the hounds bounded up the steps and a pair of gleaming jaws came together with a snap close to Lester's foot, which he drew out of the way just in time to escape being caught. Panting and almost breathless with terror the two boys crept cautiously up the roof - the moss-covered shingles were so slippery that it was all they could do to keep from sliding off among the hounds - and seating themselves on the ridge-pole looked at each other and at the savage brutes from which they had so narrowly escaped. Then they looked all around to find the person who had set the dogs upon them, but could see nothing of him.

"Where has he gone, I wonder?" said Lester, who was the first to speak.

"Haven't the least idea," replied Bob.

"Who was it?"

"Don't know that, either. It didn't sound to me like Don's voice, but it sounded like his whistle, and if it was him, I wish he'd come and call the dogs off. I am willing to give up now, Lester. Luck is always on his side, and if he will let us go home without making any fuss about it, I'll promise to leave him alone in future."

Lester could not find fault with his companion for losing his courage and talking in this strain, for he was frightened half to death himself, and he would have made all sorts of promises if he could only have climbed down from that roof and sneaked off to bed without being seen by anybody. Don did not show himself, although they called his name as loudly as they dared, and neither did the hounds grow tired and go away, as Lester hoped they would. They were much too well trained for that. It not unfrequently happened while Don and Bert were hunting 'coons and 'possums at night, that the game took refuge in a tree much too large to be cut down in any reasonable time by such choppers as they were. In that case Don would order the hounds to watch the tree, and he and Bert would go home, knowing that when daylight came they would find the dogs still on duty and the game closely guarded. The animals seemed to be perfectly satisfied when they found that Lester and Bob had taken refuge on the top of the cabin. They walked around the building two or three times, as if to make sure that there was no way of escape, and then laid down on the ground and prepared to take matters very easily until their master should come out to them in the morning. When Bob saw that, he lost all heart.

"If we never were in a scrape before, we're in one now," said he. "We may as well make up our minds to stay here all night."

"O, we can't do that," replied Lester, greatly alarmed. "Some one will certainly see us."

"Of course they will. How can we help it?"

"I should never dare show my face in the settlement again, if this night's work should become known," continued Lester, who was almost ready to cry with vexation. "It would ruin me completely, and you, too. Don and Bert would ask no better fun than to spread it all over, and your chances of carrying the mail would be knocked higher than a kite. Let's pull off some of these shingles and throw them at the dogs. Perhaps we can drive them away."

"You don't know them as well as I do. They'll not drive worth a cent. We're here, and here we must stay until somebody comes and calls them away. We'll hail the first nigger we see in the morning, and perhaps we can hire him to help us and keep his mouth shut."

This was poor consolation for Lester, but it was the best Bob had to offer. Things turned out just as he said they would. They sat there on the ridge pole for more than four hours, Lester racking his brain, in the hope of conjuring up some plan for driving the dogs away, and Bob grumbling lustily over the ill luck which met him at every turn.

At last, when they had grown so cold that they could scarcely talk, and Lester began to be really afraid that he should freeze to death, the gray streaks of dawn appeared in the east. Shortly afterward the door of the nearest cabin opened, and a negro came out and stood on the steps, stretching his arms and yawning.

"It's the luckiest thing that ever happened to us," said Bob, speaking only after a great effort. "That's the hostler. He knows me and will help us if anybody will. Say, Sam," he added, raising his voice. "Sam!"

"Who dar?" asked the negro, looking all around, as if he could not make up his mind where the voice came from. "Who's dat callin' Sam?"

"It's me. Here I am, up here on top of this cabin," replied Bob, slapping the shingles with his open hand to show the negro where he was.

"Wal, if dat ain't de beatenest thing!" exclaimed Sam. "What you two gemmen doin' up dar?"

"O, we were coming through here last night, taking a short cut through the fields, you know, and the dogs discovered us and drove us up here."

"I thought I heerd 'em fursin," said Sam; "but I thought mebbe they'd done cotch a 'coon."

"Well, call 'em off and let us go home," exclaimed Lester, impatiently.

"Dat's impossible, dat is. Dem dar dogs don't keer no mo' fur us black uns dan nuffin, dem dogs don't. Can't call 'em off, kase why, dey won't mind us. Have to go arter some of de white folks, suah!"

"Go on and get somebody, then, and be quick about it," said Bob, desperately. "And, Sam, if you can find Bert send him down. We want to see him particularly, and it will save us walking up to the house."

The negro went back into his cabin, but came out again a few minutes later and started up the road toward the house.

CHAPTER XVII

CONCLUSION

Bob and his companion were so utterly disheartened, and so nearly overcome with the cold, that they no longer looked upon exposure as the worst thing that could happen to them. They had made up their minds that it could not be avoided, and told themselves that the sooner it was over and they were allowed to leave their airy perch the sooner they would breathe easily again. They could not talk now. They could only sit and gaze in the direction in which the hostler had disappeared, and wait for somebody to come and call off the dogs. Bob hoped *that* somebody would be Bert. He was a simple-minded little fellow, and might be persuaded to believe the story that Bob had told the hostler. But Bert did not come to their relief; it was his father. When Bob saw him he wished most heartily that the roof would open and let him down out of sight.

"Why, boys, what is the meaning of this?" asked the General, as soon as he came within speaking distance.

"It means that we have been up here since midnight and are nearly frozen," replied Bob, trying to smile and looking as innocent as a guilty boy could. "We were out 'coon-hunting in the river bottoms and came through your fields, because that was the nearest way home; but the dogs saw us and drove us up here."

The General had but to use his eyes to find all the evidence he needed to prove this story false. The meal bags, in which the boys expected to carry away the stolen quails, were lying on the ground in plain sight, one of them having fallen in such a position that the owner's name, which was painted on it in large black letters, was plainly visible. More than that, under one of the planks which protected the window, was the iron lever with which Bob had tried to force an entrance into the cabin. He left it sticking there when he fell off Lester's shoulders.

"Well, you may come down now," said the General. "The hounds will not trouble you."

It was easy enough to say come down, but it was not so easy to do it, as the boys found when they began working their way over the frosty roof. The shingles were as slippery as glass, and their hands seemed to have lost all their strength; but they reached the ground without any mishap, and were about to hurry away as fast as their cramped legs would carry them, when the General asked:

"Hadn't you better go up to the house and get warm?"

"O, no, thank you, sir," replied Bob. "We'll go directly home. Our folks will wonder what has become of us."

"Are these your bags?"

"No, sir," replied Bob, promptly. "One doesn't usually carry meal bags to bring home 'coons in."

"I am aware of that fact," said the General, "but couldn't they be used to carry quails in? These bags have you father's name on them, and you had better come and get them."

These words were uttered in a tone of command, and Bob thought it best to obey. He snatched up the bags, and with Lester by his side made his way down the lane with all possible haste. When they were safe in the road, Bob drew a long breath and remarked:

"That's the end of that scrape."

"I don't see it," returned Lester. "It is only the beginning of it. Everybody in the settlement will know it before night."

"Who cares if they do?" cried Bob, who began to feel like himself, now that he was on solid ground once more. "They can't prove that we went there to steal the quails, and we'll not confess it."

"No, sir," replied Lester, emphatically. "You're a sharp one, Bob, to make up such a plausible story on the spur of the moment, but I know the General did not believe a word of it."

"So do I, but what's the odds? Let's see him prove that I didn't tell him the truth. Now the next thing is something else; we must make up a story to tell my folks when we get home."

"Can't we run back to the house and go to bed before any of the family are up?"

"I am afraid to try it. A better plan would be to go back in the woods and build a fire and get warm. Then we'll go home, and if anybody asks us where we have been, we'll say we couldn't sleep, and so we got up and went 'coon-hunting."

"I wish we had one or two 'coons to back up the story," said Lester.

"O, that wouldn't help us any. People often go hunting and return empty-handed, you know."

Leaving Bob and his friend to get out of their difficulties as best they can, we will go back to Godfrey's cabin and see what the two boys who live there are doing. The day of rest, which Don said would work such wonders in David, did not seem to be of much benefit to him after all. He had been somewhat encouraged by Bert's cheering words and the knowledge that influential friends were working for him, and, like Bob Owens, he had indulged in some rosy dreams of the future; but that short interview with the young horsemen who met him in the road below the General's house, reminded him that he had active enemies, who would not hesitate to injure him by every means in their power. He thought about his father all day, and wondered if there was anything he could do that would bring him back home where he belonged, and make a respectable man of him. He had ample leisure to turn this problem over in his mind, for he was alone the most of the day. As soon as he reached the cabin, Dan, who acted as if he did not want to be in his brother's company, shouldered his rifle and went off by himself; and it was while he was roaming through the woods that he made a discovery which did much to bring about some of the events we have already described.

Dan felt so mean and sneaking that he did not want to see anybody, if he could help it; and when he accidentally encountered Bob Owens and Lester Brigham in the woods, he darted into the bushes and concealed himself. He watched them while they were watching Don and Bert, and when he saw them hitch their horses and creep along the fence in pursuit of the wagon, he suddenly recalled some scraps of a conversation he had overheard a few days before. He knew that Lester was working against David, and believing from his stealthy movements and Bob's that there was mischief afoot, he followed them with the determination of putting in a word, and perhaps a blow, if he found that David's interests were in jeopardy. He saw every move the two boys made. He was lying in the bushes not more than fifty yards from them, while they were watching Don and Bert put the captured quails into the cabin, and when they went back to the place where they had left their horses, they passed so close to him that he caught some of their conversation. When they were out of sight and hearing Dan arose and sat down on the nearest log to make up his mind what he was going to do about it.

"I'll bet a hoss you don't steal them quail nor set fire to the cabin, nuther," said he, to himself. "Thar's a heap of birds in thar - seems to me that they had oughter ketched 'most as many as they want by this time - an' they shan't be pestered; kase if they be, what'll become of my shar' of them hundred an' fifty dollars? It'll be up a holler stump, whar I thought it had gone long ago!"

Dan knew that if Lester and his friend had any designs upon the cabin and the quails that were in it, they would not attempt to carry them out before night; but the fear that something might happen if he went home again troubled him greatly, and he resolved that he would not lose sight of the cabin for a few hours at least. He did not know what he would do to Lester and Bob if he caught them in the act of trying to steal the quails; that was a point on which he could not make up his mind until something happened to suggest an idea to him. While he was sitting in his place of concealment, thinking busily, he heard a rustling in the bushes and looked up to see one of Don's hounds approaching.

In the days gone by, before Dan became such a rascal as he was now, he had often accompanied Don and Bert on their 'coon and 'possum hunting expeditions, and the old dogs in the pack were almost as well acquainted with him as they were with their master. Bose recognised him at once, and appeared to be glad to see him.

"I want you to stay here with me till it comes dark, ole feller," said Dan, patting the animal's head. (He never kicked the hounds, as he did the pointer. He knew better.) "If them fellers comes we'll make things lively fur 'em. You hear me?"

Dan waited almost twelve hours before he had an opportunity to carry out the plan he had so suddenly formed. When he became tired of sitting still and began to feel the cravings of appetite, he went into the woods and shot four squirrels which Bose treed for him. These he roasted over a fire and divided with his four-footed friend. When it began to grow dark he went back to his hiding-place, where he remained until he thought it time to take up a new position. This was by the side of the road, and a short distance from the big gate, which opened into the lane leading to the negro quarters. There Dan lay for almost four hours, stretched out behind a log, with the hound by his side. He saw several negroes pass in and out of the gate, and, although some of them walked by within ten feet of him, no one saw him, and the well-trained hound never betrayed his presence by so much as a whimper.

Finally, to Dan's great relief, the lights in the General's house were put out, then a door or two was slammed loudly in the quarters, and after that all was still. Dan had grown tired of watching and must have fallen asleep, for he knew nothing more until a low growl from the hound aroused him. He was wide awake in an instant, and having quieted the animal by placing his hand on his neck, he looked all around to see what it was that had disturbed him. He heard footsteps in the field on the opposite side of the road, and presently two figures appeared and clambered over the fence. They crossed to the gate, which they opened and closed very carefully and went down the lane.

"Them's our fellers, Bose," whispered Dan, who was highly excited. "They've got bags slung over their shoulders, an' they think they're goin' to play smash stealin' them birds of our'n; but me and you will see how many they'll get, won't we?"

As soon as Bob and Lester were out of hearing Dan arose, and holding the hound firmly by the neck with one hand he opened the gate with the other, and moved noiselessly down the lane toward the quarters. His plan was to make sure that Bob and his friend had come there to force an entrance into the cabin in which the quails were confined, and if he found that that was their object, he would make a pretence of setting Bose upon them. He did not intend to do so in reality, for he knew the dog too well. The animal always did serious work when he began to use his teeth, and Dan didn't want either of the young thieves killed or maimed. He knew that if he could excite the hound and induce him to give tongue, the rest of the pack would be on the ground in two minutes' time; and as they were all young dogs (Carlo was shut up in the barn every night to do guard duty there), they would not be likely to take hold of the boys, if left to themselves. They would not permit them to escape, either. They would surround them and keep them there until morning, and that was what Dan wanted. He could not afford to watch the cabin every night, and he thought it would be a good plan to give Bob and his friend a lesson they would not forget.

That the prowlers had come there to force an entrance into the cabin, was quickly made plain to even Dan's dull comprehension. He saw them try the door, and then go around to the other side of the building and attempt to pry off the planks that covered the window. Dan heard something crack as Bob laid out his strength on the lever he was using, and believing that the thieves were on the point of accomplishing their object, he uttered a loud whistle to let the rest of the pack know that they were wanted, and shouted:

"Here they be! Take 'em, fellers! Take 'em down!"

Bose, who had been growing more and more impatient every moment, was quite ready to obey. Uttering a loud yelp, which was almost immediately answered by the rest of the pack, he raised himself upon his hind legs, and struggled so furiously to escape that Dan was obliged to drop his rifle and seize him with both hands. But when the brute was thoroughly aroused, it was hard to restrain him. The thick, loose skin on the back of his neck did not afford Dan a very good hold, and almost before he knew it, Bose slipped from his grasp, and bounded toward the cabin. At the same instant, a chorus of loud bays sounding close at hand announced that the rest of the pack were coming at the top of their speed. Bob and Lester had never before been in so much danger as they were at that moment.

Dan, who began to fear that the plan he had adopted for protecting the quails was about to result in a terrible tragedy, was very badly frightened. He stood for a few seconds as if he had been deprived of all power of action, and then caught up his rifle and took to his heels. He ran as if the pack were after him instead of Bob and Lester, and never slackened his pace until he was out of hearing of their angry voices. He crept home like a thief and got into bed without arousing either David or his mother. But he could not sleep. He was haunted by the fear that something dreadful had happened down there in the quarters, and that there would be a great uproar in the settlement the next morning. He felt that he could never be himself again until he knew the worst, so a little while before daylight he put on his clothes, slipped quietly out of the cabin and bent his steps toward the big gate near which he had been concealed the night before. By the time he reached it there, was light enough for him to distinguish objects at a considerable distance, and we can imagine how greatly relieved he was when he discovered Bob and Lester perched upon the ridge pole of the cabin. At first, he thought his eyes were deceiving him, but a second look told him that there was no mistake about it. He would have been glad to know if either of them had been injured by the hounds before they got there, but that was something he could not find out just then. They had not been torn in pieces, as he feared, and that was a great comfort to him.

"They never had a closer shave, that thar is sartin," thought Dan, as he turned about and trudged toward home. "I wonder what pap would say if he knowed what a smart trick I played onto 'em! I wish I could go an' tell him, but I am a'most afeared, kase he must be jest a bilin' over with madness. He's lost the pinter - I reckon Dave must have stole him, kase I don't see how else he could have got him - an' I don't keer to go nigh him ag'in, till I kin kinder quiet his feelin's by tellin' him some good news 'bout them hundred an' fifty dollars."

The events of this night were the last of any interest that transpired in the settlement for more than two weeks. Affairs seemed to take a turn for the better now, and the boy trapper and his two friends were left to carry out their plans without any opposition. Bob and Lester kept out of sight altogether; but they need not have been so careful to do that, for the General was the only one who was the wiser for what they had done, and he never said a word about it to anybody. They could not even muster up energy enough to go out of nights to rob David's traps; and perhaps it was just as well that they did not attempt it, for they might have run against Dan Evans in the dark. The latter spent very little time at home now. He was sometimes absent for two days and nights, and David and his mother did not know what to make of it. He had built a camp near the field in which the traps were set, and there he lived by himself, subsisting upon the squirrels and wild turkeys that fell to his rifle.

Things went on smoothly for a week, and during this time David and his friends were as busy as they could be. Quails were more abundant than they had ever known them to be before. They seemed to flock into the General's fields on purpose to be caught, and before many days had passed, it became necessary to fit up another cabin for the reception of the prisoners. In the meantime the General's timber and nails were used up rapidly. The boys had the hardest part of their work to do now, and that was to build a sufficient number of coops to hold all the birds. Silas Jones said that the Emma Deane was expected down every day, and Don declared that the birds must be shipped on her when she came back from New Orleans, if it took every man and woman on the plantation to get them ready. She came at last, and Don was at the landing to meet her. He held a short interview with her captain and Silas Jones, who was freight agent as well as express agent and post-master, and when it was ended he jumped on his pony and rode homeward as if his life depended upon the speed he made. When he arrived within sight of the field where the traps were set, he saw his brother and David coming in with another wagon load of birds.

"How many this morning?" asked Don.

"We have enough now to make fifty-five dozen altogether,"

replied Bert.

"Hurrah for our side!" cried Don. "We'll ship them all. Some may die on the way, you know, and that man must have the number he advertised for. Captain Morgan will stop and get the birds when he comes back. He will see them shipped on the railroad at Cairo, and all we have to do is to be sure that the game is at the landing in time."

"Did he say how much it would cost to send them off?" asked David.

"No. He will put in his bill when he comes down again. He carries freight by the hundred, you know. He will pay the railroad charges, too, and add that to his own bill."

"But what shall I do if both bills amount to more than ten dollars?" asked David, with some anxiety.

Don did not seem to hear the question, for he paid no attention to it. The truth was he had arranged matters so that David would not be required to use any of his ten dollars. Silas Jones was to foot all the bills and pay himself out of David's money when it was forwarded to him by the agent at S -, the place where the quails were going. But Don couldn't stop to explain this just now. He told his brother and David to make haste and put the quails into the cabin; and when that was done and they came into the shop, he set them at work on the coops. There was much yet to be done, but they had ample time to do it in, with more than a day to spare. When the next Wednesday night arrived fifty-five dozen quails, boxed and marked ready for shipment, were at the landing, waiting to begin the journey to their new home in the North, and Don carried in his pocket a letter addressed to the advertiser, which Captain Morgan was to mail at Cairo.

The boys camped at the landing that night to keep guard over their property. They pitched a little tent on the bank, built a roaring fire in front of it, and in company with Fred and Joe

Packard, who came down to stay with them, passed the hours very pleasantly. The Emma Deane came up the next afternoon, and when the freight had been carried aboard and she backed out into the stream again, David drew a long breath, expressive of the deepest satisfaction. His task was done, and he hoped in a few days more to reap the reward of his labor.

The boys felt like resting now. They had worked long and faithfully, and they were all relieved to know that their time was their own. Don and Bert paid daily visits to their bear trap, hunted wild turkeys and drove the ridges for deer, while David stayed at home and made himself useful there, until he began to think it time to hear from somebody, and then he took to hanging about the post-office as persistently as ever his father had done. Finally, his anxiety was relieved by the arrival of the first letter that had ever been addressed to himself. He tore it open with eager hands, and read that the quails had been received in good order, and that the money, amounting to one hundred and ninety-two dollars and fifty cents, had been paid over to the agent from whom they were received. David could hardly believe it. The man had paid him for the extra five dozen birds; he was to receive forty-two dollars more than he expected; and there had been no freight charges deducted. David could not understand that, and there was no one of whom he could ask an explanation, for Don and Bert had gone over to Coldwater that morning, and were not to be back for a week. He had a long talk with his mother about it that night, and when he went to bed never closed his eyes in slumber. Every succeeding day found him at the landing waiting for his money, and so little did he know about business that he could not imagine who was to give it to him.

At last the Emma Deane came down again. David stood around with the rest and watched her while she was putting off her freight, and having seen her back out into the stream, was about to start for home, when Silas Jones came up and tapped him on the shoulder.

"Don't go away," said he. "I want to see you." David waited an

Harry Castlemon

hour before Silas was ready to tell him what he wanted of him. By that time the most of the hangers-on had dispersed; and when the last customer finished his trading, Silas stepped behind his desk and opened his safe.

"There it is," said he, slapping a package of greenbacks on the desk and then holding it up to David's view. "How do you like the looks of it?"

David's eyes opened to their widest extent. He had never seen so large a package of money before. He looked hastily about the store to see if Dan was anywhere in sight, and was greatly relieved to find that he was not. There were three, or four men standing by, and they appeared to be enjoying David's astonishment.

"Is - is it mine, Mr. Jones?" he managed to ask.

"Some of it is, and some of it is mine. There are a hundred and ninety-two dollars and a half here, and twenty-eight of it belongs to me. Freight bills, you know. The coops you put those birds in were as heavy as lead. If you had put less timber in them your expenses would not have been so heavy."

"Don thought it best to have them strong, so that they would not be broken in handling," said David.

"That was all right. Now let me see," added Silas, consulting his books; "fifty-five dozen live quails at three fifty per dozen – one ninety-two, fifty; less twenty-eight, leaves one sixty-four, fifty. Just step around here and sign this receipt."

David obeyed like one in a dream. He put his name to the receipt, and, scarcely knowing what he was about, thrust the package of money which Silas handed him into his pocket and walked out of the store.

"There goes the proudest boy in the United States," said the grocer.

Yes, David was proud, but he was grateful, too. He was indebted to Don and Bert for his good fortune, and he was sorry that he could do nothing but thank them when they came home. He went straight to the cabin, and to his great surprise and joy found his mother there. She was alone in the house, but David, profiting by his past experience, made a thorough examination of the premises before he said a word to her. Having thus made sure that Dan was not about, he pulled out his package of greenbacks and laid it in his mother's lap.

There was joy in the cabin that day. If David had never before realized that it is worth while to keep trying, no matter how hard one's luck may be, he realized it now. We will leave him in the full enjoyment of his success, promising to bring him to the notice of the reader again at no distant day, in the concluding volume of this series, which will be entitled THE MAIL CARRIER.

Choose from Thousands of 1stWorldLibrary Classics By

A. M. Barnard
Ada Leverson
Adolphus William Ward
Aesop
Agatha Christie
Alexander Aaronsohn
Alexander Kielland
Alexandre Dumas
Alfred Gatty
Alfred Ollivant
Alice Duer Miller
Alice Turner Curtis
Alice Dunbar
Ambrose Bierce
Amelia E. Barr
Amory H. Bradford
Andrew Lang
Andrew McFarland Davis
Andy Adams
Anna Sewell
Annie Besant
Annie Hamilton Donnell
Annie Payson Call
Annonaymous
Anton Chekhov
Arnold Bennett
Arthur Conan Doyle
Arthur M. Winfield
Arthur Ransome
Atticus
B.H. Baden-Powell
B. M. Bower
Baroness Emmuska Orczy
Baroness Orczy
Basil King
Bayard Taylor
Ben Macomber
Bertha Muzzy Bower
Bjornstjerne Bjornson
Booth Tarkington
Boyd Cable
Bram Stoker
C. Collodi
C. E. Orr
C. M. Ingleby
Carolyn Wells
Catherine Parr Traill
Charles A. Eastman
Charles Dickens

Charles Dudley Warner
Charles Farrar Browne
Charles Ives
Charles Kingsley
Charles Klein
Charles Amory Beach
Charles Hanson Towne
Charles Lathrop Pack
Charles Whibley
Charles Willing Beale
Charlotte M. Braeme
Charlotte M. Yonge
Charlotte Perkins Stetson
Clair W. Hayes
Clarence Day Jr.
Clarence E. Mulford
Clemence Housman
Confucius
Cornelis DeWitt Wilcox
Cyril Burleigh
D. H. Lawrence
Daniel Defoe
David Garnett
Dinah Craik
Don Carlos Janes
Donald Keyhoe
Dorothy Kilner
Dougan Clark
Douglas Fairbanks
E. Nesbit
E.P.Roe
E. Phillips Oppenheim
Earl Barnes
Edgar Rice Burroughs
Edith Van Dyne
Edith Wharton
Edward J. O'Biren
Edward S. Ellis
Edwin L. Arnold
Eleanor Atkins
Eliot Gregory
Elizabeth Gaskell
Elizabeth McCracken
Elizabeth Von Arnim
Ellem Key
Emerson Hough
Emilie F. Carlen
Emily Dickinson
Enid Bagnold

Enilor Macartney Lane
Erasmus W. Jones
Ernie Howard Pie
Ethel Turner
Ethel Watts Mumford
Eugenie Foa
Eugene Wood
Eustace Hale Ball
Evelyn Everett-green
Everard Cotes
F. H. Cheley
F. J. Cross
Federick Austin Ogg
Ferdinand Ossendowski
Francis Bacon
Francis Darwin
Frances Hodgson Burnett
Frances Parkinson Keyes
Frank Gee Patchin
Frank Harris
Frank Jewett Mather
Frank L. Packard
Frank V. Webster
Frederic Stewart Isham
Frederick Trevor Hill
Frederick Winslow Taylor
Friedrich Kerst
Friedrich Nietzsche
Fyodor Dostoyevsky
G.A. Henty
G.K. Chesterton
Gabrielle E. Jackson
Garrett P. Serviss
Gaston Leroux
George A. Warren
George Ade
Geroge Bernard Shaw
George Durston
George Ebers
George Eliot
George Gissing
George MacDonald
George Meredith
George Orwell
George Sylvester Viereck
George Tucker
George W. Cable
George Wharton James
Gertrude Atherton

Grace E. King
Grace Gallatin
Grant Allen
Guillermo A. Sherwell
Gulielma Zollinger
Gustav Flaubert
H. A. Cody
H. B. Irving
H.C. Bailey
H. G. Wells
H. H. Munro
H. Irving Hancock
H. Rider Haggard
H. W. C. Davis
Hamilton Wright Mabie
Hans Christian Andersen
Harold Avery
Harold McGrath
Harriet Beecher Stowe
Harry Houidini
Helent Hunt Jackson
Helen Nicolay
Hendrik Conscience
Hendy David Thoreau
Henri Barbusse
Henrik Ibsen
Henry Adams
Henry Ford
Henry Frost
Henry James
Henry Jones Ford
Henry Seton Merriman
Henry W Longfellow
Herbert A. Giles
Herbert N. Casson
Herman Hesse
Homer
Honore De Balzac
Horace Walpole
Horatio Alger Jr.
Howard Pyle
Howard R. Garis
Hugh Lofting
Hugh Walpole
Humphry Ward
Ian Maclaren
Inez Haynes Gillmore
Irving Bacheller
Israel Abrahams
Ivan Turgenev
J.G.Austin

J. Henri Fabre
J. M. Barrie
J. Macdonald Oxley
J. S. Fletcher
J. S. Knowles
J. Storer Clouston
Jack London
Jacob Abbott
James Allen
James Andrews
James Baldwin
James DeMille
James Joyce
James Lane Allen
James Lane Allen
James Oliver Curwood
James Oppenheim
James Otis
James R. Driscoll
Jane Austen
Janet Aldridge
Jens Peter Jacobsen
Jerome K. Jerome
John Burroughs
John Cournos
John F. Kennedy
John Gay
John Glasworthy
John Habberton
John Joy Bell
John Kendrick Bangs
John Milton
John Philip Sousa
Jonas Lauritz Idemil Lie
Jonathan Swift
Joseph A. Altsheler
Joseph Carey
Joseph Conrad
Joseph E. Badger Jr
Joseph Hergesheimer
Joseph Jacobs
Jules Vernes
Julian Hawthrone
Julie A Lippmann
Justin Huntly McCarthy
Kakuzo Okakura
Kenneth Grahame
Kenneth McGaffey
Kate Langley Bosher
Kate Langley Bosher
Katherine Cecil Thurston

Katherine Stokes
L. A. Abbot
L. T. Meade
L. Frank Baum
Latta Griswold
Laura Lee Hope
Laurence Housman
Lawrence Beasley
Leo Tolstoy
Leonid Andreyev
Lewis Carroll
Lewis Sperry Chafer
Lilian Bell
Lloyd Osbourne
Louis Hughes
Louis Tracy
Louisa May Alcott
Lucy Fitch Perkins
Lucy Maud Montgomery
Lydia Miller Middleton
Lyndon Orr
M. Corvus
M. H. Adams
Margaret E. Sangster
Margaret Vandercook
Margret Penrose
Maria Edgeworth
Maria Thompson Daviess
Mariano Azuela
Marion Polk Angellotti
Mark Overton
Mark Twain
Mary Austin
Mary Catherine Crowley
Mary Cole
Mary Hastings Bradley
Mary Roberts Rinehart
Mary Rowlandson
M. Wollstonecraft Shelley
Maud Lindsay
Max Beerbohm
Myra Kelly
Nathaniel Hawthrone
Nicolo Machiavelli
O. F. Walton
Oscar Wilde
Owen Johnson
P.G. Wodehouse
Paul and Mabel Thorne
Paul G. Tomlinson
Paul Severing